PRAISE FOR
SHOW ME WHERE THE HURT IS

"Hayden Casey is an incredibly inventive, big-hearted writer, and his *Show Me Where the Hurt Is* is an absolute delight. There's so much joy and wonder on every page here, so much humor and heartbreak in every finely made sentence and every keenly observed detail. A fantastic debut from a writer I can't wait to read more of in the years to come."
 —Matt Bell, author of *Appleseed*

"Haunting, affecting, troubling, honest. These are the inevitable words of book jackets. But this is no hyperbole. Hayden Casey has written a masterful collection that hits every note. For an assortment of stories about people who don't know where they belong— they hit awfully close to home."
 —Tatiana Ryckman, author of *The Ancestry of Objects*

"*Show Me Where the Hurt Is* surprises and delights at every turn. I was impressed by the symmetry of the stories here; wandered along and plucked at every new fruit, which was always just as delicious as the last. The work is compelling and deeply enjoyable. Quite a few times I wondered aloud: how did he do that? This book is terrific and Hayden Casey is a fabulous writer."
 —Kristen Arnett, author of *Stop Me If You've Heard This One*

"*Show Me Where the Hurt Is* is a beautiful story collection not just about people, but about the wistful, shimmering spaces between them. Hayden Casey magically makes visible the invisible longing between us and those we love but don't understand, or worry we have lost, or hope to claim or recapture, or simply hope to be seen by, a fraction so well as Casey sees us."
 —Caitlin Horrocks, author of *Life Among the Terranauts* and
  The Vexations

SHOW ME WHERE THE HURT IS

SHOW ME WHERE THE HURT IS

STORIES

HAYDEN CASEY

Published by Split/Lip Press
PO Box 27656
Ralston, NE 68127
www.splitlippress.com

ISBN: 978-1-952897-43-6

Cover Art: Fernando Gonsales/Unsplash.com
Interior Element: Rawpixel.com
Cover and Book Design: David Wojciechowski

Editing: Pedro Ramírez

A wound gives off its own light
surgeons say.
If all the lamps in the house were turned out
you could dress this wound
by what shines from it.

—Anne Carson,
The Beauty of the Husband

CONTENTS

TO DOWNLOAD OR STREAM

THE ALBUM INSPIRED BY THE BOOK,

VISIT HAYDENCASEY.CO/SHOWME

BROKEN OPEN

My new client: Seth, 37. In his photo, he's just graying, the way the edges of a black feather glow pale in light. On the bus ride to his apartment, I study his fact sheet, on which he's outlined some basic info. He's further in the city than I am, just north of the bay—I can get there in two buses, fifty minutes. According to the sheet, he sees this period in his life as a hitch in the road: his ex-fiancée, he reckons, will wake up and realize what she's forsaking soon. They usually think this.

Fact sheet tucked into my pocket, I climb off the bus, wander up Meridian. Morning storms have given way to a brief parting of dark clouds; silvery ones slide out from beneath, allowing fragments of light to dart down. The streets and concrete are still wet, but dry patches poke through like spotted dog fur. At the base of the street, near the bay, a few shuttered mom-and-pop shopfronts sit barren, a couple specialty restaurants fluttering with activity, with noise and scents.

Seth's house is halfway up the block from the bus stop; one of his neighbors is out in the yard, knee-deep in soil. An overalled kid sprints around from the back, hands him a trowel, which he shoves into the earth. I smile, recalling a memory of our family's first garden. It had been a foul time, my sister and I dragged outside, both of us at that ripe age when we'd rather do anything but help our parents, but now it has that softness of a thing looked back on. So much softens in time.

A sleek blue Prius is parked in his driveway. I step beneath a vined arch, follow the walkway to his porch. Knock, knock—the door parts from its frame, reveals him standing behind. In person, his face is slightly different: my breath hitches as I mistake him for someone else. So easy, those slips. But no, it's him, the man I studied all the way up here, who I learned the best I could, memorizing his fact sheet like a dating profile, a half-knowing. Our clients choose us, we don't choose them, though, looking at Seth, I'm mildly pleased. He's generally attractive, blue-eyed, with a shine in them that a photo can't capture. A tall build, with a slight puff of stomach at his middle. The milky skin of a born-and-bred white Seattleite, the kind of virgin skin that would sizzle and burn were the clouds to part entirely. I soften, suddenly—I want to slather sunscreen on him, set a hat on his head, to keep the light away.

He introduces himself, like I don't already know him. He calls me Summer, the fake name on my profile, and waves his hand behind him, opens his house to me. Please, he says, halfway between a command and a plea, make yourself at home. The first day is always awkward. *Make yourself flexible*, the employee manual says. But he knows how these things go: most clients do, by now. The company has gained traction, and I'm, more often than not, a repeat hire.

I step into the house, and the sound of my footfall volleys around the room like a hollow ball. His place is tastefully decorated, with floors of dark rich hardwood and long vibrant runner rugs down the halls, in dark colors and creams—a woman must have done it. Want a tour? he asks, waving me back. It's a single-story building, with high ceilings, a cluttered guest room—Don't mind my mess, he says, keeping the door mostly closed—and halls full of portraits. Sure enough, there's a woman prominent in several photos: they stand together in large empty fields, on golden beaches, in wide yards. In some, they hold each other at a distance, like siblings; in others, she's dipped in his arms, like a poster for a TV dancing competition. That's Stephanie, he says.

She looks like me, I say. I don't mean to verbalize it, but I do.

A little bit, he says, in a tone that admits more than he lets on. That's one of the things that drew me to you, he continues. That, and your personality—what I could gather from your profile. He gestures toward the living room. Please, he says, take a seat. Can I get you something to drink? Water, soda, liquor?

No thanks, I say. In the manual: *Alcohol use is discouraged, unless the client insists. Avoid becoming visibly intoxicated or allowing your judgment to become impaired.* I'll have a drink later, I'm sure. I lower myself onto his couch, new leather, still stiff. I keep quiet: *Allow the client to establish the atmosphere they desire*, the manual says, meaning: Allow the client to clutter the air with talk, if they so desire, but don't do it yourself.

He asks me about myself: Something not on your profile, he quips. The manual says, *Come up with a story and stick to it. The less of your true self you give away, the easier you'll be able to release the client upon contract expiration.* Dark, I suppose, but practical. I launch into a false story about growing up in the area, about a best friend that got married last year. As I speak, he sits and listens, watches with genuine intrigue.

He smiles, wry, at the end of my tale. What? I say.

He says, None of that was real, was it?

I blanch. No one has ever called me on it before. Either they believed me, or they wanted to buy into the illusion so bad, they looked beyond—I'm not sure anymore.

It's OK, he says, I get it.

He turns his face away from me, glances around the room, at the high ceilings and beams and pale wall paint he's seen a thousand times by now. Anything not to look at me. It's just, he says...I don't know why I thought it'd be....

I can feel myself losing him—I can feel his belief in the company, in its mission, slipping. My stomach seizes—I don't want this loss. My track record is sublime, spotless; my evaluations are iron-clad. I won't allow myself to lose.

So I leap into something else, something real, and sentence by sentence, I recapture his intrigue: it's the best feeling in the world, a direct rush, his eyes on me. He listens, keeps listening.

We're called Personal Transition Mediators. In-Betweeners, they call us on the streets. The role is designed to bridge the gap between relationships, to supplement the empty, lonely space with something resembling intimacy, for those who have the means. *You'll never walk alone*, a company billboard says. In a bind, in need of quick cash: as they say, a job is a job. Staring down my late twenties—never too late for a new direction. I tore a tab off a streetside flyer, typed the company name into the search bar. You're perfect for this, my roommate Maria said when she saw the slip of paper on the dining table, you're a stone-cold bitch. I pretended to be offended, but I understood what she meant: I have broken but I have not broken open. Some parts of myself are still contained—I can hold most of myself intact, mind the gaps. What she also meant was: I am good at being used, good at shaking it off afterward, to an extent.

The interview was full of fascinatingly invasive questions: *When was the last time you were in a relationship? How did your last relationship or otherwise romantic entanglement end, and who do you believe was at fault? How long, in months, would you say you spent mourning its end? How have friends and family described you? How have past romantic partners described you? On a scale of one to ten, how strongly do you relate to the following identities: Hopeless romantic? Obsessive? Confident? Detached? Strong-willed? Metamorphic? Happy?*

I wondered which of these answers could function as a red flag. Regardless, I passed—I was approved, added to the site's inventory.

All I had to do was set up a profile and wait as offers rolled in. And they did, in what felt like moments: sessions with all sorts of people, mostly men.

It's not sex work, they'd be quick to add, it stops just short. The manual says: *We have utmost faith in your ability to morph.* **Be the person your client needs.** *Some of our clients are looking for pure companionship; others opt for something that more closely resembles romance. Take your client's temperature, and adjust accordingly. But remember: sexual contact is expressly forbidden.* Some of the men, a manager warned us in an early group meeting, will want to take it further, but the contract is strict. It'd be a breach, an immediate termination. Don't let it happen—don't feel like it *has* to happen. They know the rules too. If you're ever in a gray area, just come talk to me.

A coworker, Maeve, huffs in her seat next to me when the presentation ends. You can tell a bunch of fucking men run this place, she says—no rules in place for protection. How long till the first lawsuit? She holds her hand out, and I set my phone in her palm. She plugs her contact information in. If you ever need it, she says. We'll throat-punch some fuckers.

I've been OK, in most cases.

What I tell Seth is about my sister, Maggie, how she's my favorite person in the world. How I never see her anymore, because she's renounced the West Coast and lives on the other side of the States, but how I wish I could see her every day. How the truest parts of my life, the parts that sunk in the deepest, the parts that felt most like memoir chapters, were the parts in which we spent time together. How, as girls, a year and a half apart, we played dress-up, shared clothes, spun stories, used our dolls to imagine our futures. The present we find ourselves in: neither of us had imagined this. How, as teenagers, we went to the same parties, made the same friends, played on the same soccer team. How she wasn't always as pragmatic as she is now, how we were once the same.

As I speak, the living room has become populated by versions of Maggies, from all phases of her life: Artistic Maggie, when she found herself captivated by senior-year art class and briefly surrounded herself with paint and canvas, spread newspapers all over her bedroom floor, wore borrowed smocks around the house; Studious Maggie, away at college, her slender shoulders bent over a desk with a textbook spread open, a six-pack of Red Bulls in her mini-fridge; Hippie Maggie, when she started dating Julien and lost herself a bit in his strange aromas, his captivating carefreeness.

What do you think changed? Seth asks at the end of the story. If you've always been so close, he says, how could she move so far away? He catches himself, reddens a bit, starts again. Sorry—I phrased that badly. What I meant was....

No, I say, I get it. I chew on my lip, try to stop tears from spilling over. The versions of Maggie I've conjured disappear, one by one, fading back into memory. The last time she saw me, tears obscured her own vision: dozens of me must have swum in her eyes, a kaleidoscope of sister.

I don't know, I say. That's all I can get out. Some things still stop me in my tracks—some wounds still hurt like they're fresh.

He sets a hand across mine, and the contact startles me, wakes me. Thank you, he says, for sharing that. You didn't have to.

But I *did* have to, I think to myself, or else tomorrow, you would've terminated our contract, and I would've been paid for one session, shipped off to the next client. I had to open myself, to win you over, to keep you. *Be the person your client needs.* I had to be exactly me.

He looks down at our fingers, interlinked, startles at the sight, like he hadn't noticed it either: Is this OK? he asks. I'm unsure whether he's asking on a personal or a contractual level, but there's another softening in me at his consideration. I nod, smile.

He pulls his hand away and sets it back on his knee; mine goes cold, exposed to air. He lets out a breath, large as the whole house. I know we were supposed to go longer today, he says, but if it's OK with you, I think I'll let you go early. You're great, and I'm excited to see you tomorrow, it's just—I've had a long week, I'm really tired, and, this whole thing, it's—I mean, you're great, I just think I need to....

The client reserves the right to book sessions as he or she pleases, the manual reads, *and to modify booked sessions 24 hours in advance, to avoid a late cancellation or modification fee.*

You're fine, I say. That sounds perfect. I'll see you tomorrow. Let me know when.

All communication with the client must happen within the Connex platform, the manual reads, *where safety can be monitored. Avoid giving out or collecting personal contact information.*

I won't put the change in, he says. You get paid more that way, right?

He doesn't really care—he's only trying to dodge a fee. I nod, smile, again.

As he shuts the door, a pleasant smile overtakes him, and out of the corner of my eye, I swear to God it's Julien. Rub the half-dark out of my eyes, look closer, and there he is, grinning from within his Carolinian camper van. What he means, the prickle in my eye, the hot flood of emotion in my stomach—I push it down. Not now.

In our off hours, we gather at the office, write up timecards, leave brief session comments. The workspace is crushing—plain gray, boxy, soulless as a stock photo. I've just opened Seth's file, left an opening comment: *more perceptive than past clients. will have to keep an eye on his pursuit of honesty/openness, he can see through my lies.* I delete this last sentence—some things those up top don't need to know.

A new coworker at a neighboring desk eyes my name card, wiggles her eyebrows. *Summer,* she says. That's a smart pick. A lot of these people around here are really desperate for summer.

I nod, smile. I fall into patterns of doing this. Her name card reads *Carmen.* Exotic, I say.

My real name's *Agatha,* she says with a groan. They were like, *We'll only hire you if you go by something else. Like, anything else.*

I smile, continue typing.

She asks, Do you have a type yet?

I think back across all my clients. Not really, I say.

She groans. For some reason, she says, I'm a fucking incel magnet. All the emotionally stunted men-children who've been single since college see my profile and are, like, *You, please*. She mimes an excited pointing gesture. Whatever, she says. Money is money. Better they spend it on me than…I don't know, PlayStation tokens or something. What's sadder: buying girlfriend practice or buying video game money?

My first client: Jay, 29, a deep-leered flirt. His girlfriend finally left him for good after three years of on-and-off chaos. Sometimes he sent me home early, in anticipation of a hookup, having fulfilled his emotional need for the day. Curled up together during movies, he loved to keep a hand gently set on my stomach—I love, he said, to feel you breathing. It was like lying against a plank of wood; I'd never felt a torso that muscular.

He woke each night two, three times, calling out in terror. *Dad*, he said, *Dad*. I had to coddle him, calm him down, stroke his back like that of an anxious dog.

My second client: Marc, 28. Gay ("Got my gold star right here!," he'd bragged), and he'd recently lost his lifelong female best friend in a car accident. I need you to make up some drama, he'd say. All my coworkers are so fucking boring, and Abby always had the tea.

So I stroked my chin, like I was inventing something juicy, and gave him something real: the story of my sister and her ex-boyfriend. Holy *shit*, he said—naughty, naughty!

He slid over cash, sometimes—a handful of twenties, or a hundred, if he had one. We weren't allowed to accept tips: anything we garnered had to be deposited in the company's bin, like a church's collection box. The next morning, at the office, I'd slip his cash in—I was still a good worker, then.

*

My third client: Leah, 31, freshly disentangled from her first relationship with a woman. Some of their photos still lined the walls—I was a dead ringer for her ex. The split had been recent—half of the physical space was still bare, divots still set in the carpet from the furniture her ex had taken. She called me by her name, stroked my cheek with her thumb. *Some will grieve like this,* the company had warned me—*some will try to replace what they have lost, and it's not your job to guide them, to lead them elsewhere.* She'd recently dyed her hair a pale gray that brought out the red in her skin, made her look constantly sunburnt—her straw-stiff strands brushed at my shoulders like horsehair. We watched *But I'm a Cheerleader* every night. She laughed at the same jokes each time. Her laugh reminded me of my sister's.

Everything hurts, she said.

Welcome to the club, I said.

The next afternoon, Seth and I are on opposite sides of his kitchen island; he's at the border between stories. We've talked for hours, as the light has risen higher, and conversation has come easy—it's not a ruse, this time. He's got a couple orange bulbs lit above us, a pan set on the stovetop—he's glopped some olive oil in, set a low flame for it to warm.

I've been cooking eggs in olive oil lately, he says. I can't get them to crisp the same way in butter. I guess it's about flavor versus texture.

He asked me, a few minutes ago, what I wanted to eat, and the honest answer slipped out before I could hold it back: fried eggs on toast. I reddened, thought of the manual—*Do not impose upon clients; remember,* you *are the hired party*—and backtracked, said we could eat anything he felt like. He laughed, pulled a pan off the rack hanging from the high ceiling. Order received, he said.

Really, I say now, you don't have to make anything, I can do it.

Or we can order out, anything you like.

It's OK, he says, grinning. You're a human being—I'm gonna treat you like one. And you made a good call—eggs sound really good. He turns toward the fridge, pulls a tan carton of eggs out, sets it near the pan. His blue button-up, still office-crisp, is coming untucked toward the back of his belt line; a wedge of late-thirties hip-pudge pokes out. From here, I can't reach—if I stood, walked around the counter, I could slide my fingers beneath, tuck it all back in.

Do not get attached, the manual reads. *The client reserves the right to terminate his or her contract at any time. Do not allow this to sting.*

When the oil shimmers, he cracks a few eggs in the pan and they sizzle, seize up at the sides, solidify. He turns around, catches me looking at him. I lower my eyes to the bowl of fruit at the center of the island—I can't tell if it's real or fake. Lemons, limes, oranges. I reach out and touch, skimming them with my fingertips. Plastic— could've fooled me. Look just like the real thing.

What do you think of me? he asks out of nowhere.

Remember only what is necessary to maintain conversation, the manual reads. *This will make the disentanglement process quicker and simpler.*

What do you mean? I ask.

Sometimes, he says, you look at me a certain way, and I can't tell what it means.

What kind of way?

That's what I can't figure out. He uses his spatula to slice between the eggs.

You remind me of somebody, I say, finally.

Who? he asks, sliding bread into the toaster, lowering the levers.

Julien washes over me: his blue eyes, pale as spring water, his slender limbs, skin soft and moleless. His bare back, across the couch in his camper van, like a glass of milk knocked over. The checks I send, month after month, to Maggie, to help with his rehab bills.

Somebody I haven't seen in a long time, I say.

He senses the wall I've put up, doesn't dare to tap at it.

When the eggs are done and the toast is crispy, he slides them across two plates, cracks salt and pepper on top, sprinkles parsley across for color. I run my knife through the eggs, sitting at his table, and the yolks break open and run across the bread, yellow and velvety. I feel his eyes on me; my skin warms.

Good? he asks.

Perfect, I say.

Stephanie loved eggs, he says. I learned how to make them just how she likes them.

She's not dead, you know, I say. You don't have to speak about her in the past tense.

We've talked about most things but her. His eyes have softened—maybe I've touched a nerve. I set my fingers over my mouth, fear I've crossed a line, but he shakes his head, forgives me.

No, he says, I know. She's said she was gonna leave a few times before. But something about this time was…different.

We eat in quiet for a few breaths—just the sound of knives scraping porcelain, teeth touching forks.

He then asks, Do you ever think, *This is fucking sad?*

My brows slope downward. Huh? I ask.

Not you, I mean. He looks around the room. But—this. This whole thing. I'm literally paying for, like, pretend intimacy.

Discuss the company in positive language, the manual says. *Do not disrespect the company or its mission.*

A little sad, I say. And not you, either. But more just its general existence. I mean, it makes sense that someone would pay for this, if they were able. The guarantee of it.

Even if it's false, he says. Even if it's all false.

He then skirts my wrist with his thumb—my stomach begins to burn over a low flame. I pretend I don't feel it. But, he says, something about this doesn't *feel* false. I don't know. Maybe it always feels like this. Maybe it's what I'm paying for.

Maybe, I say. After a short while, I run a fork tine through the plate's congealed egg yolk, scoop it all up.

He laughs. I can wash the plate, you know, he says.

Zero waste, I say.

He stands when I've finished, carries our plates to the sink, soaks them. He reaches for a bottle of wine then turns toward me, like I've caught him at something.

TV? he asks. It's five o'clock somewhere.

Looking at him from the table, a truth strikes me: he will, I know, tap at the wall—gentle, at first, then more firmly—and he will break through.

My fourth client: Mahmoud, 33. His girlfriend had announced her desire to move back to Iran to be with her parents and ailing grandmother, and he'd scrambled, terrified, given her a foolish ultimatum. Now his closet and bathroom cabinets were half-empty.

How could I have done that? he anguished. Idiot, idiot. His wrists trembled, like he was restraining himself from striking his own head.

He was a wonderful cook, spoiled me with lavish meals, richly flavored meats and rices. When I left his apartment, I smelled of cardamom and rose water. He never wanted to touch. When I woke in the mornings, he was kneading dough for komaj, though he never cared for it—his girlfriend had loved it, and he enjoyed the slight sound of pleasure I made the first time I bit into it. When he made us tea, he left a third cup out, as if she might walk in at any moment. A little pot of cream, though neither of us took it.

My fifth client: Philippe, 42, a classy, dignified Frenchman and fresh divorcé who loved to shower me with gifts, jewelry, spending money. He kept me prim and manicured like a little purse-sized dog. Muzzled, touchless.

Mon ex-femme, he said, didn't feel like I valued her—can you imagine?

He embraced his natural odor, loved to smother me in it. His pit-stink stuck to my skin, took three scrubs to get off. When his contract expired and he didn't renew, I pawned the bracelets and rings, the thick gilded watch, and stayed jobless for a while, lived off the thousands, sent some of it for Julien.

This piece of salmon, I told myself, setting a rice-bedded flake on my tongue, was worth half a loop of that silver chain.

My sixth client: Frank. Not much to say. He set his hand on my thigh, and I said, I think you've got the wrong idea about this whole thing. He said, The customer's always right. I slicked out from beneath him, slid out his front door. I flagged him in the system, had him blacklisted. He made a new account, left me a one-star review: *bitch. don't bother.* My boss had it purged from the site, but I still have its screenshot stored in my computer. It was my phone wallpaper, for a while.

And lucky number seven: Seth. He doesn't tell me about Stephanie, and I don't give him the real meat of myself. In this way, we each keep a bit of ourselves from the other.

But still, some things crop up in my head: how Julien invited us on a camping trip, once, just me and Maggie. He thought it would be a good way for us to get to know each other, better than a single meal or an afternoon at home. They'd been together for two and a half years at that point—they'd met at school in North Carolina, and I hadn't yet visited her there. He'd come home to meet our parents once, but I'd been at school.

I was used to the drier West—I stepped out of the airport, and my hair swelled to twice its usual size, the air in my lungs thicker, my skin fogged with wet like I was always fresh from the shower. Julien took me in his arms the first time I met him, held me tenderly for several seconds—Lovely to meet you, he said, taking me in. You're certainly Maggie's sister, aren't you.

He began every morning with an hour of silence, spent in yogic concentration: reading or sipping coffee or just looking at the van's wall, tracing the lines in the wallpaper. He lit incense, kept several mantras at the tip of his tongue, reminded himself of them often. Sometimes, walking by, I caught him whispering to himself.

Holy shit, I said to Maggie: what planet is he from?

She went sullen, looking at me.

He was an addict, she says—this is his way of moving forward. He dressed in loose garments— baggy pants, oversized shirts, wore necklaces and bracelets that glinted in the sun. I understood what drew her to him: beauty, every level of it. I held restraint, or tried to, so I wouldn't sink into it myself.

Over the long weekend, we hiked, built fires, listened to the radio, drank cooler-chilled beers. The trouble began on the last night when the weed came out. Maggie shook her head, scrunched her nose up, but Julien and I carried a small pipe out into the dank woods, passed it back and forth between us. In the firelight, the years-old track marks in his arms glowed bright; my eyes gravitated toward them, tried to read them like letters. The weed woke an appetite in me—my fingers found his skin, traced the raised patches.

I wore long sleeves, he said, for the first few months, so Maggie wouldn't see—it took me a long time to unpeel myself.

My eyes watered; it was a detail I found beautiful.

And it was in the thick wet forest that I brought his scars up to my mouth, tongued them.

I see it coming, yet I'm helpless to stop it. Or so I tell myself. Wine or refusal of wisdom or pure want, who's to say. Sitcom reruns on the screen, hollow laugh tracks bouncing between Seth's high ceilings.

Are you comfortable? he asks. His leg tucked between mine, a blanket thrown over us. Twin glasses of wine on his coffee table, a deep red sip left in each. Poke bowls, ordered for delivery, scraped clean, soaking in the sink. The evening outside gone black. His heart lurches against my right shoulder blade, taps at the bone.

Yeah, I say, you? I shift back against him, the slightest motion, and his stomach hitches—I feel him harden, a cell at a time. The length stretches up my lower back. I shift my hips again—he exhales, sends a rush of breath down my neck. My heel skims his shin, the hair there. His bicep over my breast, hand tucked in my arm, pulse in his wrist tick-ticking away. I take his hand, guide it down my stomach. His muscles seize—he knows the rules.

The manual says, the manual says—I don't care what the manual says.

It's OK, I say.

Further, down my sweat-slick skin, beneath the waistband of my sleep shorts, every inch grows more intense. His arm, beneath my head—I turn toward it, bite, to keep from crying out. Circles and circles, fingers sinking deep and retreating, splaying out and retracting like tentacles. Physical sensation, to push memory away. Eventually I throw a leg over him, and he pulls the rest of me atop.

I settle, I sink.

Maggie had fallen asleep by the fire, slouched over in her camping chair. Julien pulled the van door open, slinked up the steps with his slim limbs, and I followed him inside—the dark swallowed us up as the door swung shut. Bright with our new appetites.

I wasn't supposed to do this again, he said. *All the best things, I'm supposed to stay away from.*

Seth says things to me, on the verge of wine-weighted sleep, earnest slurred things like: Even if I'd just seen you, I think, just out on the street somewhere, I think we'd have found each other. Like: I don't know what I expected when I signed up for this thing, but it wasn't this. Like: How is this happening? Like: Where have you been?

Julien and I planned our confession: only a kiss, a half-truth, half-lie. To get the satisfaction of a confession but keep the dirty truth between us. We discussed specific wording, blocked out the scene:

who had initiated, who had given in.

It turned out our confession wasn't necessary—we stepped out of the van and found Maggie had abandoned her fireside seat. In the far distance, we saw a flashlight beam cast across the trailside, wobbling across the forest floor. We sprinted toward her—she'd wanted to walk down the hill, toward the far-off town, but underestimated the distance and eventually just crumpled to the ground, gave up. When we caught up to her, she was sobbing and initially refused to return to the campsite with us, but after a while, jaw clattering away from the fire, she relented. We dragged her back to the fire, and she was illuminated: spit dribbled down her chin, tear-streaked cheeks, fall leaves caught in her curls.

I flew back home the next day, switched my flight to the earliest I could find. Maggie didn't answer any of my texts afterward.

When Julien relapsed, I sent my sister a check. *For rehab*, I wrote on a sticky note I tucked into the envelope.

All the best things, he'd said, *I'm supposed to stay away from.*

I'd opened the floodgates.

I expected the letter to bounce back, but it didn't. The money was pulled out of my account. I couldn't figure out what was best: to remove myself from their lives, or to try to help. So I did what felt best. I began to send these checks monthly.

Am I telling Seth any of this, or only thinking it? In the flashing blue light of the TV—it doesn't matter. I feel his breath, the rise and fall of his belly, the warm slick of his air. I am bringing him closer to what he wants—I am helping him, in this way.

I wake before the sun, Seth asleep beside me. My phone is buzzing, over and over—I ignore it, shove it into my pocket, poke out the front door to catch the bus out of the west. On the bus, I keep my gaze pointed out the front windows to keep from hurling. I nearly miss my stop; I pull the cord moments before the bus passes it. The driver veers into the lane, catches it just in time. Julien in my eyes.

The week before Seth booked me. Three missed calls from Mom, late the prior night, and a text: *Call me when you get this.* Seven more calls after that, in the early stretch of morning. A voicemail, two voicemails. *I don't know where the hell you are,* she says, *but you need to call me. Julien died yesterday. Somebody snuck something into the facility and he got a hold, and his heart gave out. They found him on the bathroom floor. You know how it is—once an addict, always an addict. Jesus. Rest in peace. Call your sister.* The voicemail ended.

I navigated to Maggie's text thread, which had gone green instead of blue—she'd blocked me. I called once, twice, to confirm. Nothing.

At home, I find a new email on my phone. As I read it, I sigh a large sigh of relief: Seth has terminated our contract.

Floating above the wine headache, I'm giddy, like a child on Christmas morning. We can leave the land of the contrived, enter the land of the real. I bounce around my apartment, throw the curtains and windows open, let in the sound of summer storms, the sloshes of car tires, of torrents in gutters, the sound of an uncontrolled heart.

I've been a bad employee. I know this, and yet, what choice do I have? What everyone asks themselves when they've crossed some line, can no longer see it drawn behind them. I can act as surprised as I want at where fate has taken me, but I know it's been built into me this whole time: this breaking, hard-wired.

But unlike last time, I've got someone to gather the pieces, to reassemble them.

I show up on Seth's doorstep with a stuffed duffel bag, a dog-shine in my eyes. He guides the door open, shirtless; water droplets gather at the unshaven edge of his chin, surprise cutting through the sleep in his eyes.

I was hoping it'd go this way, I say. You canceled the contract— and thank god for that. You wanna get out of this city and so do I: Let's go somewhere. Just for the weekend or, I don't know, maybe longer.

Then, footsteps from down the hall. A woman appears behind him with a hotel-white towel wrapped around her, skin wet from the shower, curls bundled into a bushel on top of her head: the woman from all the photos he still hadn't taken down. My stomach sinks.

Come with me, I plead to him. Come with me.

Who's this? the woman asks.

He freezes—he can't provide my name, because he doesn't know it. I plugged my name into his phone under *Summer*, but he must have known it wasn't real.

So he turns back toward me, expectant.

HOT YOGA

My roommate, Matteo, leaves a note on the kitchen counter where we keep the mail.

GONE TO CALIFORNIA, it reads, MOTHER DIED. His half of the sink is clear of dishes, his side of the coffee table free of books and papers. Bedroom door open, room tidy.

I send messages, leave courteous voicemails—I'm so sorry, are you OK, text me when you get there. He doesn't answer them. On my fifth try, before his tinny automated voicemail prompts me again, I feel a vibration against my bedroom wall and stand to investigate. Down the hall, in his room, his phone is plugged in on his nightstand, buzzing against the wall, my name on the screen.

A few days later I come home from class and find him in the kitchen, digging through the produce in his drawer. A stack of folded paper grocery bags sits at the edge of the counter. His hair, long and curly these days, is pulled back with a band. I wait, but he doesn't acknowledge how the trip had been, how he is doing, just continues to rustle. I am afraid to ask, afraid to open the lid of something I cannot close. I have always been bad at voicing things.

Fruit is scattered across the counter—blueberries, strawberries, blackberries—out of their clamshells and in small bunches around the blender. He chews on the seeds as he tosses the berries into the pitcher, precise in the wrist, like he is sinking ping-pong balls into Solo cups. The seeds are snug between his teeth when he smiles at me, his hand on the blender's dial.

This is gonna be loud, he warns.

A pair of packages comes with his name on them. He lugs them into the kitchen as I lift a forkful of spaghetti to my mouth, my last bite of food for the day. He smiles as he opens the packages: in the first is a trio of yoga mats, black, blue, and pale purple; in the second, a stack of DVDs. He lifts a mat, banded with thick paper, to his face and scrunches his nose at the scent.

That's what Subway bread is made of, I say.

He laughs, flattens the boxes, and wedges them between the trash can and the wall. He sets the DVDs on the console by the TV, then disappears to his room with his mats. I leave my door open, hoping to catch him on the way to get water or food, but he remains in his room for the rest of the night.

Matteo has been here before, in the shallow pool of his grief—I cannot remember what I did last time. I was in a pool of my own then, my world split open like a peach. I am unsure of how to straddle the line between being compassionate and affording him distance. I worry I am doing neither.

He was my younger brother Noah's best friend. They grew up together, Matteo's house a mile from ours, and when they entered undergrad, I offered them the two soon-to-be-open bedrooms in my apartment. Were they rowdier, it would have been a bad idea, but they'd gotten all the mischief out of their systems in high school. They were quiet and respectful, if not entirely tidy. Matteo, sister-less, was unsure about living with a girl, but Noah assured him that I kept to myself. And I did, and I do: to class, to the library or the café, to bed.

My interactions with Matteo were always filtered through Noah: when Matteo joined Noah and me for dinner, hiked with us, came with us to tour campus after Noah's and his acceptances. Everything I learned of Matteo I have watched Noah pull out of him one piece at a time, and over the years, I have formed a composite of his character. Noah unspooled him, untangled his fraught wiring. I wished for a friendship like theirs, tightly knit even when they had girlfriends, even when Matteo had boyfriends.

Matteo's never been much of a talker: he is an only child, has a very only-child way of dealing with things. He shoulders alone what he doesn't want to confide to others. When the two of us found ourselves suddenly alone here, we shut ourselves in our rooms, rarely broke the silence. Now the apartment is a cold thing, and each of us pays more rent so Noah's room can remain as it is. Neither of us go in there. My mom came once, right after it happened, to go through his room, but now when she visits, she meets me outside the apartment, can't bear to face it.

I come home from class and Matteo is doing yoga in the living room. He has pulled one of the rugs back, pushed the coffee table against the couch, laid a lavender yoga mat out across the tile. An instructional video plays on the TV, helmed by a ponytailed blonde in a sea-green shirt. Her face is vaguely familiar from afar.

Hold that pose, she says. *Breathe with me. Listen to my breaths. Do you feel that?*

I feel it, he says, his words hoarse from his position. He is splayed out on the mat in gym shorts, his dark hair against the rubber. The

TV is louder than normal—I can hear not only the instructor's fin-ger-taps of words, but her breaths, her motions across her mat.

I feel it, he says again. I watch the thin dip in his back as he stretches, watch it sink and lift.

Hey, I say.

Hey, he says. Don't mind me. Back to the TV he says, Yes, I'm here, I'm here.

I step around him and walk into my bathroom, where I wash my hands, dirty from clutching my bike handles. I keep my eyes on my hands in the mirror, do not raise them to my face, my arms. I hear the instructor through the door: *If you're wiped after this workout, it's the perfect time to whip up one of my Revive smoothies. Find that recipe in my "Healthy Blends" book—it's just what I'll need after this.*

Back in the kitchen, I notice a flower on the counter: a rose, white, stripped of thorns. I brighten slightly, though I don't allow myself to smile.

Where'd this come from, I ask, running a finger along its smooth emerald stem.

He tilts his head up toward me.

Someone gave it to me on campus, he says, neutral, as if it were an everyday occurrence.

Part of me is surprised to hear he was on campus—that he had left the apartment at all—but I nod. How many opportunities have I been given to ask him something, anything, that I haven't taken?

I'll probably just throw it away, he says.

My face, I'm sure, reddens, but he doesn't notice. He shifts, following the instructor up onto his knees, beads of sweat shining at the ends of his curls.

At night, when Matteo has gone to bed, I wander, a slow step at a time, out into the kitchen. The flower is still on the counter. I pick it up and bring it back to my room. In the dark, I twirl the flower in my fingers, lift it to my nose. I pretend it was handed to me: someone stopped me, looked at me, extended a flower between the fingers. I pull the velvety petals off the stem one at a time, white and soft as cream, and eat them. In my empty stomach, the petals sit heavy.

He is practicing yoga most mornings when I leave and most afternoons when I come home. A question about his coursework rises in me—I haven't seen an engineering-related thing in his space since he returned from California—but I am afraid to ask. Noah wouldn't have been afraid—he would have leapt right in, suave as a diver.

Instead of speaking, I sit at the dining table and watch him proceed to slowly eat three crackers. His flexibility has increased—he is now able to follow the instructor through poses that involve near-splits, incomprehensible bodily curvatures. In his black shorts, he holds poses with marbled stillness.

Another package arrives a week after the first, this time a trio of recipe books, which he tucks beside the microwave. The trash is always full of strawberry hulls, the sink always loaded with knives and the dirtied blender shell. Since his return, he eats nothing but smoothies; I worry he is wasting away. He has always been skinny, but now, in his complex bends, his ribs are protuberant, his shoulder blades sharp beneath his skin.

Your form is excellent, I eventually say, though I know nothing about yoga. The words sag in the air, ring cheap with falsehood.

Thanks, he says. I've got the best teacher there is.

The one on the TV? I ask.

Yeah, he says. Have you ever done yoga?

No, I say.

Truth be told, I have always found it amusing—the silliness of the bends, the intense focus, the participants who regard it with such graveness—but watching Matteo, it begins to make sense: the calmness in his limbs, even when they support him in unnatural stances; the placidness in his expression when he returns to a normal position; the satisfaction it seems to give him, visible in his lax eyes, his loose cords of shoulder, the slowness of his breaths. His hair now falls nearly to his shoulders.

One of my exes used to do yoga, he says. And I used to laugh at her. But it turns out she was onto something.

He puffs out his bottom lip, exhales, blows the hair out of his eyes. It launches upward, settles in among the rest atop his head.

You might want to try it, he says. I have three mats, you know.

I laugh. I just might, I say. Though in truth, the thought of my body in those configurations, the skin that would show, tenses me like a violin string.

He faces forward, interprets my non-committal response as a no, returns his focus to the screen.

A warm night, right after Noah died. Matteo and I had turned to parties, started to understand why people fell so willingly into them. We had just stumbled back into the apartment, sent the Uber driver off with a hefty tip and a series of profuse thank-yous, and shut the door behind us.

We floated into the kitchen, drank large gulps of fridge-cold water, ate slices of plain bread out of the bag, in the pale flickering of the stovetop light. He drifted down to the floor, somehow graceful, and, looking up at the ceiling, blinking with those shiny drunk eyes of his, said something sweet and melodramatic, something corny in retrospect but a kick to the gut in the moment: I wish every night felt like this.

I didn't know what *this* meant but I was warm in the glow of his reverence for it. I thought back, still half-drunk: the sky had opened above us and we had all run inside from the backyard; the way he hovered at my shoulder like a bug; then the lovely drive back afterward, the lingering smell of the rain.

I sank onto the floor next to him, gracelessly. He laughed at the thud I made as I hit the floor. Half a slice of bread on the counter, a fruit fly swimming in the stove light. Everything was formless.

At one point Matteo said, Hey.

I turned toward him. He was closer than I thought, and for

just a second, he set his mouth against mine. Extended his tongue, brushed my lip: gentle, tender. An inquisition.

It was at that point I pulled back, disentangled from sensation and he remembered where he was, who this was. He seemed to come to his senses.

Oh my god, he said, his mouth still at my nose, his breath stinging like a shot of vodka, Fuck, I'm so stupid. He fell back, eyes angled up at the lights in the ceiling. He stood and went to his room, left me on my side on the kitchen floor.

I don't know what he saw in me: a trick of the light or a drunken illusion. Maybe he saw Noah in my nose, in the color of my eyes, and confused that recognition, warm and familial, for something else.

I used to walk into the apartment and find him bent over the kitchen table, eyes inches from his engineering textbooks, poring over them. These days I find him in the same spot in front of the TV, contorted on his mat. The sun has long set, the blinds all still open, and the orange-bulbed streetlights fill the room with dusk. The TV casts its blue-white LED sheen onto him, onto his mat, his legs outstretched before him.

Matteo, I say with a laugh, what are you doing?

Almost done, says the instructor on the TV.

Matteo pants something under his breath, something I can't hear.

Huh? I say, trying to project my voice over the TV's volume.

Whew! There we go, the instructor says. *Let it all go. Doesn't that feel good?*

Matteo releases from his foothold, allows air deep in his lungs. He breathes for a few moments before he acknowledges me again, turning toward me.

I got an academic status report today, he says loudly.

What? I ask.

I've missed too many English classes, he says. I'm going to have to withdraw.

Feel that relaxation, the instructor says, *deep in your core.*

My eyes bulge. Are you serious? I ask.

Painfully serious, he says.

Breathe with me, the instructor says.

Why aren't you going to class? I ask.

Do you want to do yoga with me? he asks.

Why aren't you going to class? I ask again, louder.

I shift my gaze to the TV, really look at it for once, squint at the brightness. *I'm Annette DiFranco*, the instructor says, standing swiftly from her position on her yoga mat. Her studio is wood-floored, white-walled, well lit. *Thanks so much for spending time with me today.* The camera zooms in on her face, and she smiles at me.

My stomach drops out. I recognize the smile, the dimpled cheeks, the prominent canines, the lip curvature: it's Matteo's, it's all Matteo's.

I'm spending time with Mom, he croaks, his eyes gleaming in the LED light. The video has ended, gone back to the DVD's silent menu screen, and all that remains is the static hum of the ceiling fan. Her face, her grin, shines on us.

She misses me, he says.

When Matteo has finally called it a day, somewhere in the soggy space past midnight, I walk over to the TV and pick up the stack of DVDs. *Annette DiFranco: Faith in Flexibility*, parts one through seven. She beams up at me from the cover, dressed in pink, hair in its familiar knot. As a child, I'd never seen her, only the tinted sheen of her car window as she came to drop him off or pick him up. I properly met her for the first time when she helped him move into the apartment. She was so generous, I remember, so kind with him. I think of her features, her large milky eyes and sharp jaw, now echoed in Matteo, and wonder how I didn't recognize her in the DVDs earlier. Perhaps because she was so far away; it wasn't until the camera zoomed closer that recognition washed over me.

In the months after Noah died, when Matteo and I were ghosts of people, he only seemed alive when she called. He told her things he didn't tell me—about his friends and classes and late nights, about the changing lives of his high-school classmates. His laugh, through the wall, surprised me: it poured from him like sun.

I wake up parched, suddenly alert, at three a.m., and head to the kitchen to get water. In the hall, I hear something blaring from Matteo's room. Light spills through his partway-open door. I inch toward it: he lies asleep in his bed, a bare arm draped across his eyes. Every one of his lights is on.

An interview with his mother plays on his laptop next to him, at full volume.

I love the work, of course, she says, b*ut at the end of the day, I love coming home and being with my family.*

I shut it, and he shifts in his sleep, rolls over. I turn off his lights, his bedside lamp and his corner lamp and his ceiling-fan bulbs, close his door, fill a cup with water.

Back in the dark of my room, I google her for the first time. The resulting articles are all about her death: the shock of it, the sorrow. A multi-car collision on a stretch of lonely highway. In one of the included pictures, on a tabloid's website, she's with her family: her husband (separated now), and a small Matteo, no older than four, his hand clutching at the hem of his mother's skirt.

The DVD won't come out, he says.

We are in the living room a few days later. He has just finished the fifth disc in the series; Annette's other series, *Fit, Free, and Happy,* is on its way to him in the mail. His ribs are further exposed; he is still dwindling. I feel envy, then a twinge of guilt: it doesn't seem to consume his thoughts the way it does mine. He doesn't count his steps, his bites, his meals. A series of large boxes have come to him via UPS, substantially heavier than those with the yoga mats. He has dragged them through the doorway, left them along the wall of the front room. I haven't eaten yet, only had coffee, and my stomach grumbles beneath my laptop. I have half-paid attention to him, half-studied. It takes effort to look away from him.

The DVD won't come out, he repeats.

Try again, I say.

I did, he says, his tone sharp. He jabs the button on the DVD player again and again, with increased force, until the DVD player scoots back into the cubby.

Did you try the remote? I ask.

I don't know where it is, he says.

Did you look for it? I ask.

No, he says.

Why don't you look? I ask.

Because this should *work*, he shouts.

Hey, I say.

But it's *not fucking working!* He then rips the DVD player out of the wall, severs it from its cords, and hurls it across the room. It crashes into the blinds, which clap hollowly against each other, and falls to the floor, where the DVD player splinters into pieces, plastic and metal, black and silver.

Then he is sobbing, heavy and slobbery, like a child. Curls into himself, arms around bony knees. I set my laptop aside, meet him on the floor. Hold his head in my hands, think of every reassuring thing I have ever heard, say them all to him. He is drooling on my shirt. This is the closest I have been to him since the night on the kitchen floor. I lose my breath, we are so close. I try not to think about his elbows tucked into the flesh at my sides, try not to think about the wingbeats in my ribs. He shudders like a breeze passes through him. His skin is hot, his hair sweat-slickened against my shoulder.

I want to bring up the night after the party. My throat clasps around the words, holds them in—maybe he has forgotten it, or it will reopen some wound. We sit there rocking together on the tile floor as he starts to calm down. From the front of the DVD box set, his mother looks down at us.

As we sit there in silence, my tongue softens: I want to tell him, finally—the way I feel, thinking of him on the other side of the wall, hearing him laugh. Waiting for him to come home; the way, when he finally opens the door, something settles inside me and I feel some sense of resolution. The words bubble in my throat.

I told her not to come, he says in the newfound silence. His voice is deep, worn.

What do you mean? I ask.

My mom, he says.

Not to come where?

Here. She wanted to come here. She wanted to come see me and I told her not to. She decided to come anyway, to surprise me. And look—look what happened.

I cradle him, stroke his head with its soft bundle of hair. He feels like a child, collapsed and weak, bones jutting through skin.

Eventually he peels away from me and I sit in the middle of the floor for some time, reeling and sweat-slicked, soaked through at the underarms, swallowing down the words I hadn't gotten out.

He sleeps late the next day, past noon, comes with sleep-sewn eyes into the kitchen for coffee. He drives to the Target down the street, comes back with a replacement DVD player. His mother's second DVD set arrives in the afternoon, and he slices open the box and slides the first disc in, runs to grab one of his mats. When he turns to me, he seems almost startled by my presence—asks me, with the unenthused tone of an afterthought, if I want to join him. I say no, content to sit and watch him. The air conditioner kicks on, metal rattling against metal.

He hasn't shaven in a while, and the facial hair is jarring on him, incongruous, like a toddler wearing a stick-on mustache. He sits across from me at the kitchen table—his broom-thin arms, bent at the elbows, jut out of his shirtsleeves, head propped against fists.

His hair is long, touching his shoulders when it isn't pulled back.

I withdrew from English, he says. I might have to drop out.

Are you serious? I say around a small bite of cereal, chewed eleven times and swallowed. A bit of chastisement in my voice, like I am his guardian looking at his report card.

Yeah, he says.

What are you gonna do? I ask. I have no idea how he is getting money, for all this fruit, for all these packages. The entryway has become difficult to navigate, boxes propped atop boxes—when I asked him earlier what was inside them, attempted to lift one of them, he said, *The future.*

I'll be OK, he says. He is bright, eyes clouded with preoccupation, as he looks over at the wall of boxes. His conviction is nearly convincing.

After I eat and shower I look at myself in the mirror. Really look, good and hard, for the first time in a month or so. I have made progress: my stomach has receded, my jaw has inched out, become more pronounced. Still there are sections of myself that I can't stand, that I pinch at as if I can will them away with my fingertips. But it is a start.

On campus, in the window of time before class begins, I wander the immediate buildings, look for people handing out flowers. I remember the white petals, how they felt on my tongue. Every time I turn a corner, I think, This is it, they will be around the bend, waiting for me. But my face goes red with shame: it was an opportunity long missed, long gone. I return to my building, trek up the stairs to my classroom.

Matteo texts me: SURPRISE WHEN YOU GET HOME. Knots form in me, unspool. I try to suppress the racketing in my chest, the sad bit of hope that flurries up, but it's no use. My imagination leaps ahead of me. Maybe he will have flowers for me; maybe he sees me.

When I return home, there is a sign on the front door, handwritten in thick Sharpie: HOT YOGA. A blast of heat strikes me as I open the door—a heat I haven't felt since summer ended—and then a wave of whirring sounds. The living room has been emptied, the couch and coffee table shoved into the kitchen. The boxes that lined the walls have been opened and unpacked: space heaters and humidifiers churn around the room. Seven people sit on yoga mats, spread out on the floor, their eyes all fixed on Matteo, kneeling in the front in a sea-green tank top, his dark hair pulled back behind his head. They slowly turn to me, registering me as a vaguely threatening presence.

For a moment I can only look: at the strangers, their water bottles and mats, shoes and drawstring bags; the machines, the thin wispy trails of the humidifiers. Then I see Noah's door down the hall, wide open, the empty boxes cast into the darkness of his room. Something in me splits in two. There is a stack of flyers on the floor in the doorway: HOT YOGA, it reads, then, in smaller print, WITH ANNETTE DIFRANCO'S SON.

Something else bubbles up in me, something I haven't felt this hot and thick in years: fury, at the heat, at the crowd, at the open door down the hall. Over the onslaught of whirring, I say, What the hell?

Matteo seems pleased, with all the eyes on him, in his mother's colors, his mother's postures—he seems so happy. Welcome, he says, paying no notice to the storm of emotions in me. Join us, won't you? His dark ponytail swishes at his shoulders.

Why is Noah's door open? I shout. A fog of heat has washed over me, soaked my underarms, prickled at my hairline.

He notices my mood and a conciliatory instinct rises in him: Come here, he says, rising from his mat, stepping into the hallway. Excuse us, he says to his pupils.

I follow him into Noah's room and my stomach churns, seeing my brother's bed, sheets taut, my shoes sinking into his carpet. A chill rushes through me at the temperature shift. My soul aches: the room still smells of him.

We had rules, I spit. We don't come in here. This is his space.

I needed somewhere to put the boxes, he says. Just for now.

Don't you think this has all gone too far? I say. You won't get her back.

But it's too late: I have held my tongue too long, and I know I have lost him entirely. He has receded into her, curled up in her. I start to feel her presence in the crater of his smile, the whites of his eyes. And I look at myself, in the mirror doors of Noah's closet: I have curled up in him just the same.

I already have, Matteo says. Isn't it beautiful? His eyes, glass-shiny, say he no longer needs to be helped.

And I have to thank you, he says. You've felt, these days, just like a mother to me.

There it is: a sharp cavern of hurt in the stomach, a sting in the eyes. Though I knew how he felt—I must have known, somewhere—it still tears me open. He's misinterpreted my care for him, misunderstood what I wanted, interpreted my doting as maternal, not as what it is. Can he not see the feeling pooled in my eyes? Do they not plead strongly enough?

He guides me out into the hall, shuts Noah's door.

Again, he asks, Why don't you join us? He gestures to a yoga mat propped in the corner, rolled tightly, bound with elastic. Third time I ask is the charm, he says. Or maybe fourth, I've lost count.

I have done so much for him: held my tongue when it threatened to run, given him the space he needed to grieve, shoved the swelters of emotion he'd risen in me back down, time and time again. I can do this for him, too. I can be what he wants.

I take the mat he extends to me, lay it out across the floor, lower myself to the ground. Blink away the tears that have formed in my eyes.

He smiles at me, back at the front of the room. By now, he

has learned the material by heart; he no longer needs the DVDs, though they sit on the TV stand behind his head, displayed like a shrine.

I'm Matteo DiFranco, he says to the room. Thanks so much for spending time with me today.

EVERGREEN

She watches Ben kneel and sink his index finger into the soil of the date palm, his eyes narrowed in focus, as if feeling for a pulse. Two years ago, he'd told her he felt like he was moving into a nursery—setting his U-Haul boxes beside the thick bases of pots, tucking his books behind shelved plants, stepping around floorcoils of vines—but now she watches him tend the things with care, with something approaching love. He trims dead undergrowth with the thick kitchen shears, measures and levels fertilizer with a plastic teaspoon, checks the moisture of the soil with practiced indices. She watches him look back at her, smile.

Still all right, he says, before he stands and moves to the next.

Things, for now, feel OK. Comfortable. He waters the plants rotely, but pleasantly. Plants are precarious, finicky things—just when you think they are happiest, they begin to wilt. And just the same, she's been afraid. Three months ago, he told her he felt something was missing in his life, in their relationship, and her feet have felt eggshelled ever since. It has loomed over her, the Something. She wanted to scream, cry, pull herself apart: What is it that I don't have, what is it that you need that I can't provide?

He spent longer hours in his bedroom-converted-into-office on the weekends, went for longer solitary drives. She only knew he was back when she heard his music, his Frank or Erykah, falling out his open car windows. She imagined his slow walk up the steps, his hesitation at the landing, his glance over the railing to the parking lot below, the palms and hazes of clouds in the distance, his one-two-three count before he twisted the key in the lock, like he'd found that Something somewhere out there and was making the choice now to leave it behind and lock himself inside their apartment without it. She's dreamed of their inevitable end again and again, woken with river-stones of regret in her throat, clutched at him like an inflatable raft. He was still here, still here.

While she's at work, a few days later, Ben finds one of her short stories. She had printed it, left it out in the open—a silly mistake.

Erin, he says when she gets home, voice somehow breathless and booming, like she'd filled his lungs and punctured them simultaneously. You never told me you wrote stories, this is amazing. He turns the pages, ginger as scripture, and says God, this is it, this is the Something. More, more, c'mon, there's got to be more. Print more for me. He's still at her desk, in the corner of the kitchen, beaming.

She hasn't forgotten the Something, she's thought about it every day since, but to hear it aloud again stings like salt in a cut.

They have, for the first time since the early days, really great sex; he is a ravaging thing. But his eyes, she thinks, keep wandering to the bedside table, where he's set his phone, and beneath it, the short story. Or it's a trick of the moon, an untoward flicker of the TV light. He snores afterward, a light purr of a sound, as he does when he's exhausted.

In the morning, he holds the story over his bowl of cereal, eyes gliding through lines of print as he crunches.

I should be bothered, he says, because you've kept this from me for so long. But I'm just so happy I'm being let in on it. Feels like a gift.

She had never called herself a writer. She'd chosen a different path, rarely let her creative impulses out, only on weekends when Ben was away for meetings or trainings. She had forgotten the shiver-slick way it felt to have his attention. He quotes one of the lines—one of *her* lines—and she winces in misery; it's torture to hear them read back.

I mean, he says, come on, how good is that. You have more, don't you?

He turns to her, in the late hours of another night—when she thinks he's asleep and she's listening to his cycles of breathing, watching his hands folded across his sternum, tracking the fissures in his knuckles lit by fractals of streetlight—and says, eyes lit with wonder, What else have you been hiding from me?

She had been surprised he'd wanted to see her again after their first date. She'd noted, she thought, the precise moment at which the light had left his eyes, the exact second he'd lost interest. She'd tried to figure out which preceding hobby or opinion had turned him off, or perhaps she'd smiled too wide or laughed too loud. She thought of his goodbye kiss as a reluctant thing, turned it over as she fell asleep, felt the last buzzing traces of the cocktail leaving her system.

In the morning, she saw his text and she left it unopened, turned the screen on and off, allowed its buoyant light to hit her again and again.

In the early months of the relationship with Ben, her friend Claire, across the top-heavy bar table, limeless stir stick in her left hand, said: I don't know how you landed him. And Erin agreed, feverish, because Claire was right. He's unspeakable. One of those people who attracts admirers everywhere he goes, leaves legions of shiny-eyed new admirers behind. She's long known her luck, and she's been waiting for him to wake up and blink the fog out of his eyes and realize it too, to tell her this wasn't where he was supposed to be, and then take flight.

Any day, now. Only a matter of time.

The next time she saw Claire was across a different bar table nearly a year later. Claire had often, since the start of their friendship, drifted out of touch for long periods.

Claire asked, Are you seeing anyone? and Erin said, Still Ben, and she reveled in the look in Claire's eye, the sheer unfathomability, and she held onto the look for a long time, wielded it in her mind like a slick power. It wasn't a victory against Claire, per se, but a victory against the world: the unimaginable thing she had was happening, and it was lasting. She and Ben were good together. They were a good fit.

Her mother had walked out on her father when she was a senior in high school. Her sister had caught her husband with another woman's breast in his mouth. She needed to believe this thing she had spent her life chasing, that she finally believed she had pinned down, could be real.

And so she clung.

A few days later, she runs another story off on the office printer.

One at a time, from the archive; in low doses. The night before, he reread the first story before bed, muttered incomprehensible lines to himself. She fell asleep to his soft murmurs. I'm delirious, he said, This is the best thing I've ever read.

In the morning, she noticed the story hadn't even made it to the nightstand when he finished. She got up to shower and he lay there on his back, the story beneath his clasped hands, flat against his chest like it was snuggling up against him. In the middle of the night she'd woken in shivers, pulled the blankets higher, pulled them in tight, like a limb, like a body.

Do you still love me? she whispered in his direction.

He shifted in his sleep, rolled onto his side, his arms still clutching the story like they were straitjacketed there.

A third story, now, sent to the office printer. She doesn't want to think about what happens when she runs out, what Ben will become. In the morning, she'd lifted the second story to wipe the nightstand beneath it, and Ben leapt at her like she was trying to steal it. She hasn't written a new one in months, but eventually, she knows, he will need something new.

On her way to pick up the copy from the printer, her boss stops her at the door: What's this? he asks, clutching her story in his right hand. He flips through it with cigarette-darkened fingers, smiles at her with stained teeth. He straightens his tie, hands the stack over to her. Doesn't look like invoices, he says.

She fears termination—it's happened for lesser reasons here—but he says nothing further, lets her walk back to her desk.

When she enters the apartment, he is looking at her like a dog that smells meat. She lingers in his gaze for a moment before she hands him the story, and he immediately takes it to the couch. Ben has been neglecting the plants—the leaves are beginning to curl and brown at the ends, the new growths yellowing. His feet propped on the opposite chair, the spilled-ink tattoo spiraling his ankle, the slight hunch of his shoulder as his head cranes toward the open faces of pages—he is a man in love. Her soul splits open for him.

You know, she says, feeling brave. I was going to go to school for it, she says. For writing.

He doesn't look up from the story. She wonders if he is listening.

But that was when Mom got sick, she continues. She was so sick.

He laughs at something on the page. She knows he is not hearing her.

So I couldn't go, she says. But I keep trying. I don't know if I can ever stop trying.

He flips the page. She goes into the bathroom, lingers there, sighs into the sink.

If it all came to an end, Claire would hold her, pull her hair back, feed her bites of ice cream from the carton; she would help her through. But with a gleam in her eye, a smug sense of victory, because Claire had been right all along, hadn't she?

On Valentine's Day the next weekend, he wakes early, rises from the bed, goes into the other room, rummages around in the kitchen—he hasn't forgotten, she thinks, they aren't in a state of dissolution. She is tired; she was up late writing a new story for him. She rolls over, allows herself to fall into a blissful half-sleep, figures he will wake her when he is ready.

She sits up at 11:30, realizes he still hasn't come. When she pads into the kitchen, she finds him at the desk in the corner where she works, a bag of King's Hawaiian rolls open at his side, half of them gone—his jaw moves in slow motion, crushing the same bit of bread again and again. His fingers are perched over her computer's trackpad, the document of her stories open in front of him. She doesn't know how he got the document, whether she'd left the laptop open all night, whether he'd hacked his way in. Tears, she notices, are pooling in the hollows of his eyes, bubbling over onto his cheeks.

Morning, she croaks, blinking back tears of her own.

He can't just do that to her, he says. It's not fair.

She knows exactly the story he is talking about. She had been saving it for last, not because it was the best, but because it felt like the end. Because she knew it was coming, the clean cleave of it, when she had exhausted all other options and had only one last offering, and there was nothing else for him to take, nothing else that interested him. He had picked her bones clean.

He stands and steps over the pothos vines, the yellowed crisps of their leaves, on his way into the bathroom. The faucet runs—he is washing his face, wiping it clean, scrubbing the emotions away. She used to love the faraway sounds of him, wanted to hear them forever, to keep them there.

She prints everything she has for him at Kinko's and slams a heavy duty stapler through the corner. He'd barely relinquished her computer from his grip at the corner desk till she talked him down with promises of printing. Her eyes are heavy, foggy—she only caught a few hours of sleep after finishing a new story for him. She is starting to see him more and more as a deranged thing. Fuck it, she figures, he can have them. If her hold on him is going to give, let it come crashing down.

But she doesn't quite anticipate, in the coming days and weeks, the sheer degree to which he recedes into the pages. The snake plant, which is supposed to be the easiest for them to keep alive, begins to wilt; a few of its stakes bend in half, flop over onto the rim of the pot. He begins to raid their supply of packaged ramen for its convenience; she comes home to find nuclear yellow powder on the tiles, bowls crusted with dried broth in the sink. He stops showering, begins to smell like he has long been dead; the pages of the manuscript begin to yellow and crease from the sweat in his hands.

On the fourth straight day, when the soft red T-shirt he hasn't taken off has begun to darken with pit stains, when he's piled the sink with dishes and scribbled words across the manuscript pages, her tone changes. She has looked over his shoulder, tried to read the markings, but they are indecipherable, scratchings more than words, long stretching things spread along the margins. No longer is she interested in the spectacle of it, how long he could keep it going, how long he could survive. It has become solely sad, lonely: the thing she has fought so hard to keep alive is cut off at the roots.

It's like I'm not even here, she says.

I'm sorry, he says, but I'm falling in love.

But you don't show it, she says.

Not with you, he says, his eyes soft and distant. He strokes the top page manuscript, its neat, clean edge.

But the writing *is* me, she says.

No, he says. It's not.

At the end of the packet is the newest story, finished in the early hours of the morning. She watches with dread as he gathers the pages, detaches them from the packet. Not as good, he says. Feels rushed. The pages flutter to the ground, fold over each other like leaves.

She meets him on the couch, extends her hand. His eyes shoot up to hers, narrowed, like he knows what she is going to try.

Give them back, she says. She puts a hand on the manuscript, attempts to pull it from his hands.

His eyes brim with anger. No, he says. He strengthens his grip till his knuckles are white and pulls it right back toward him. He looks at her like an enemy, stalks off to read in peace.

She stays on the couch, sets her hand at the imprint his body left, the cushion still warm. She scoots into his former spot, sits in the stink of him there, hears him turn a page from down the hall.

He's a light sleeper, so her task is difficult, but not impossible. She waits till his eyes dart back and forth behind his lids, till she knows he's in REM, the manuscript curled on his chest as always. The middle of the bed, as she leans across it, is so cold. She extricates the pages, slides them out slowly from under his forearms. He shifts at one point, and she thinks she's been found out, but his eyes go back to their darting.

In the living room, she rolls the pages into a cylinder, as if to wrap them in a rubber band. Instead, she fills the watering can all the way up and tucks the manuscript into the hole at its top.

She watches the pages soak and relax, watches the double-spaced type and his ink scrawlings across the rearmost sheet loosen and disappear into the water. Only the bottom half of the manuscript will be wet, but she can flip it later. She is killing his darlings, and her own too.

She looks around at all the dying plants—such tenuous hands she had put her trust into. She has written loving onto his basic functions—coming home, watering plants, cooking meals—and has wrangled him into a loving creature; her eyes are tired from straining to see him in that light. In the morning, when she and Ben wake, she will tell him what has to happen, that he has to go. She will wait for him to come back to himself, and she will wait for him to see her.

She thinks she hears him stirring, now, in the bedroom—shuffling, feeling around for Something.

IS THIS IT

What they don't tell you: it can be any day.

On the way to work, peering at passing apartment balconies—what would it be like, you wonder, to have that window, to catch that southern light? Or to have a chair like that, suspended from a hook, swaying like a wave?—a bang sounds and you're suddenly on the ground, a cataclysm in your vision, a leg bent beneath your bike, ripped open and red-washed where your skin hit the street. But nothing much, a few cuts, a few slow trickles. Less a feeling of pain than a shift in axis, a sense that the world, which you thought faced one way, now faces another—a haze, like you're watching the whole thing from a story above.

Stars bloom behind your eyes. The girl who opened her car door into your bike lane and sent you soaring is now blubbering, having gone a bit green in the face after surveying your blood and cuts, the bits of yourself you've left along the asphalt, but you assure her, Everything's fine, it's all fine. I just wasn't watching, is all. It's fine. You intone it like a promise, right yourself and climb back atop. You *pedal on*, like your father taught you all that time ago. Were he here, he'd be proud of your dedication to your work, of all the long hours you've spent. He had always wanted to see you labor in this way, to put your degrees to good use, to chip away at your debt.

One of the last cogent things he said to you: *Follow the money.* And then he called you by your uncle's name, hurled something vaguely sexist at a passing nurse. In the word-soup of his last days, that phrase stands out to you like the one digestible line in a difficult poem—the rest, in its near-nonsense, makes the one phrase feel truer.

At work, you peer over the bathroom sink and investigate the swelling: a half-dome at your left temple, purplish, aching, like a golf ball sliced in half and glued to your head, leaking a stream of deep red. Where, you wonder, did this mass come from? You imagine the worst: a hidden crack in your skull, a slow seep of brain matter bulging behind the skin, cyst-like.

You're already late and you know your boss will chide you later. No time to deal with this now. You give yourself a half-bath with wet paper towels, scrub the blood away, wipe yourself clean. Nothing you can do about the rips in the shirtsleeves, the dark streak across your left thigh like a swipe from a tiger.

At your desk, Carson comes to drop off invoices. When he sees you, the pile of papers comes crashing to the floor. *Jesus,* he says as he scoops them up. He looks at you like—oh, right. He asks, *What the hell happened?* You say, Oh, I'm fine. He asks, *Are you sure? That looks bad.* It's fine, I'm sure. *Like, really bad.* I'm fine. *Did you get it checked out?* Yeah. *Really?* No. *Why the hell not?* I'm out of PTO. *Can't you take a few hours off anyway? I mean, if Davis saw this....* But you don't have the energy to explain that rent is due at the end of the month and you'd had the money portioned away like a good little egg, but you had to dip into it when a brick had been hurled through the car window and your wife's purse had been stolen out of it, even though it'd been tucked out of sight, and so you had to drop the car off at the shop, where they'd found other critical issues—*You really need to bring this thing in more*, they'd said, *you're lucky you even made it down here*—and you recently had to dip into your PTO when your wife had gotten it, because that's what you were supposed to do in those days when you were exposed, you were supposed to tuck yourself away for a while to make sure you weren't spreading it, and on the TV, while you approximated healing, you watched the leader of your nation-state co-sign the scattering of bombs across the ocean, caught an animated visual that softened the blow, as if it were only a child sprinkling bread atop a pond for ducks floating past, and your little girl asked, as cameras shook from explosive force, *Are they the bad guys?*, but you couldn't tell who the *they* was, so you had no words for her—and then she'd gotten it too, and it had put her through the wringer, turned her red, spotted her skin, flung her left and right in fevered dreams, pulled pained moans and whimpers out of her, and you'd have done anything in the world to siphon out that pain, to bring it into your body instead of hers, but your insurance didn't cover the meds she needed, and the manufacturers had recently ramped up the cost, and you'd had to run the heater higher to keep her body temperature from plummeting when it was wreaking its worst havoc in her, so your power bill would be higher, but it wouldn't do you any good to heat a house you've been evicted from because you couldn't pay your rent—so you say No, or you try to, and you turn back toward your monitor, which has taken on a strange fuzziness—and you're on the floor of your cubicle then—the ceiling flashes with trapezoids, tessellating in the hot light—pale as inner down feathers—maybe it's not an injury, you think—maybe it's the brain gathering all those wrongs it holds and rejecting them all at once—all the ways you have let the world down, all the ways it had let you down in return—maybe it's the brain begging for more of your goodness to leave you with—you wonder to yourself, *is this it—is this*—but you've already known it—when the light through the blinds has gone gold in the morning—moving, you are moving—when a breeze has shifted through your sweat-soaked shirt—through light red and white and blue, through siren sound—when your long-ago father has browned butter in a pan, plopped pancake batter in, coaxed you out of bed on weekends—this—when your little girl has realized the symmetry of her name, its forward-backward sameness—this, here, you know, is nothing near—this, is—this—

EVIDENTIARY

Finding out hurts the worst. The spiral of it: discovering one thing leads to another thing. It's like a film over her eyes has suddenly been lifted and she can see the world in new light.

First, a receipt, in the pouch of her husband's work bag, for gas station condoms. Liam has never gone for condoms with her: she went on the pill for him, swayed queasy through her lunch breaks, pinched at her extra waist flesh. And once, in the early days, when his nerves kept him up, they went for the morning-after pill: she imagined it dissolving inside her, spreading through her like radiation. No condoms, never condoms. The receipt sits leaden in her stomach.

Then, when he is in the shower, she cannot get into his phone. He has changed his passcode for the first time in three years. She enters the four digits she knows, his birth month and date, again and again, till the device makes her wait a few minutes to try anew.

*

It is true that sometimes she does not look. She goes to work and does her number-crunching, her mind-numbing, and she comes home and expects things to remain the same. They sit near each other on the couch in the evenings, watch cooking competition shows, spoon leftover dinner out of reheated bowls. And it is true, she can't keep up with Liam, with his urge that presses into her every morning without fail. She is tired and, eyes half-shut, she rises, leaves him to tend to his need alone. Lust is a thing that hovers in the rearview, she cannot turn back to it often. But she tries, she tries, every now and then.

And if it's true that she does not look sometimes, then neither does he: this late-morning, he steps out of the shower, towels off, walks by her, opens his drawer. She's seated at the edge of the bed with the receipt crumpled in her hand, a look on her face, she's sure, that attempts but cannot ultimately convey the emptiness she has discovered inside herself. But he does not see. He drops his towel, steps into a pair of boxers, his front turned away from her as if to preserve modesty. Frigid blue late-morning light lines his shoulders.

He speaks about his brother Calvin being back in town, how he's made reservations for a dinner for three sometime next week, but the date doesn't matter, it doesn't stick. Liam speaks to her over his shoulder, keeps his cock angled toward the wall. She waits for him to turn and look at her so she can present the receipt, but he doesn't, not once. After he dresses, he hangs his towel on its hook, leaves the room. She hears the fridge open, hears the thin metal click of a bottle cap landing on the counter.

She finds herself slipping the paper into her pocket. It seems to her like a surprise knight overtaking a rook; a surprise power play. She finds herself in a game she didn't know she was playing, a game of how long.

She decides she will let it all play out on its own. Instead of confronting Liam, she will wait for him to crumble. By then, she will

have assembled a barrage of evidence and he, standing tall and no-
ble, with the sense of having done the right thing by confessing, will
waddle away with his tail between his legs. Or so she can only hope.

She has never doubted him, never doubted their love: today's feelings are caustic and all-consuming and new. Is it all really more
valuable to him than her forehead kisses, their back-and-forths with
a glass of wine on the couch, their late-night stove-lit slow dances,
the sweet smell of her skin?

It must be, it must be. So she buys condoms, from the same
seedy gas station he visited in the shadow of the freeway overpass.
The same kind, even: she traces the abbreviated item code from the
receipt to the shelf labels. That night he starts, reddens when she
slips one from the drawer, tucked between her fingers like a ciga-
rette, but she swears she feels him firmer against her leg. After the
last scare, she says, I think we should. And it's like everything is new:
it's like the first time again, sweet as a high-school sneak. She makes
a sound she imagines the other woman making as he nips at her ear,
slips into her. She gasps like she's shocked when really she hasn't felt
anything like this in a long while. And then an earring catches in the
gap between his teeth and tugs. She yelps.

Slumped over the mirror afterward, listening to Liam loud-
breathe atop the sheets, she dabs at the crusted blood with a perox-
ided Q-Tip. She consults her various emptinesses: her stomach, her
heart, her mouth, the space between her legs. When she gets back
to bed he is asleep, and she tucks herself beneath the quilt, throws a
leg over it, hugs it like a body.

She has little need for lust, but she relies on love. It's no longer a
thing that drives her wild, keeps her up at night, leaves her sick and
dizzy, but it's something she stands atop all the same: the other body
there in the room, breathing, warm, quiet. And now, in the wake of
these emptinesses, she wonders if she ever had anything to stand

atop at all. What is the difference, she wonders, between love and comfort? What have they had for these three years, if not both?

.

He is careless with evidence, she learns, so the whole thing must have been going on for quite some time. Scraps of the other woman are everywhere: in the morning, she spies a pair of lace panties tucked into the breast pocket—the breast pocket!—of his blazer, and she slips them out, lifts them to her nose. They smell like her and not like her—some new concoction, some special heady sweetness. She imagines him doing the same thing with them as he pulls out of the driveway, sniffing, squeezing himself through his slacks. She slides into the panties and the blazer too, saunters around the house in them during her morning hour alone.

She used to sit in the kitchen, sip her coffee mournfully, wish his commute weren't so long so they could enjoy a bloodied sunrise together, so she could rub sleep from her eyes and see him there on the other side. She sits on a kitchen barstool, runs her toes along the cold floor tiles. The panties fit her hips like they're her own.

On the way to work, amid seas of tail-lights, she spins her silver band around her finger, runs through the rote script. Almost a year ago, now: happiest of near-anniversaries.

To have and to hold, they said. All she has now is a shred of receipt—every now and then she tucks her hand in her pocket, holds it, reminds herself it's real.

From this day forward, they said. At the time of speaking, he hadn't been able to comprehend that impossible distance. We all, she thinks, make promises we can't keep.

For better or worse, they said. The ups and downs, the ebbs and flows; they'd navigated it all, came out steady, or so she thought. He'd found better, in her, but he wanted best.

For richer or poorer, they said; *in sickness and in health*, they said.

And the last part, oh, the last part—hasn't the death already come, splintered them right through?

It's grief, or a sort of grief: she feels he is lost to her forever, he has been cleaved from her life completely. She watches herself cling, feels herself pull closer, hold tighter.

The next night, wine-buzzed and spun out together on the couch, when she's almost drunk enough to sabotage her long game and call him out on the receipt, and in fact feels the words bubbling up in her, he slides a hand beneath her skirt, skims the edge of her lace panties—which she's taken to wearing—and calls her by the wrong name. She doesn't quite catch what he says, the precise mess of syllables that spells out the other woman, but she holds their wrongness like an ache in her ear, a hitch in her throat. And instead of everything in her going mute, clicking off like a TV switch, she comes alive, with the new possibility of what she could be. She climbs atop, takes control—fills in what's missing from her new name, her no-name. She feels fuller for a moment. His eyes fall shut, and she knows who flashes behind them—look at me, she thinks, as I rise to that challenge.

She finally sees Liam's brother, Calvin, the week after finding out he was back in town. In truth, she had forgotten—it was only upon arriving home and seeing Liam in a button-down, the one Calvin had gotten him as a Christmas gift the year before, that she remembered his visit.

The three of them go to dinner at a restaurant they know Calvin cannot afford. Liam loves to provide, to dote on his family with gifts and plane tickets and hotels, but Calvin, following a long chain of perceived inadequacies, hates to accept handouts—he lasers in on the menu's cheapest item, restricts himself to a single glass of wine before he tapers off to water.

When Liam stands to find the bathroom, she notices Calvin eyeing her fondly. He's like her own brother by now. He holds his fork just above his plate, romaine and crouton speared on its tines.

He says, You two seem better than ever.

It is at this moment that she realizes how good she is at hiding the inner wreckage of herself. She nods, sips her wine, runs a slow finger around the rim.

First wedding anniversary soon, at the top of next month: paper. She imagines, in intricate gift wrap, beneath scissor-curled ribbon, a single receipt, handed back to Liam. What would she be able to read in his reaction? What new truth would settle into his brows?

Nothing, no matter: by accident, she realizes with an empty moan, she's run the receipt through the wash and can no longer pore over its characters, analyze its date and time, wonder if he bought them alone or with his other woman in tow. It's gone to pulp in one of her pockets, falls apart in her hands.

The other woman has an affinity for touch, she learns. She joins Liam at a work luncheon, with her heart in her throat, and it doesn't take her long to figure out which woman it is: she skirts around the room, brushes every arm with her fingertips.

Of course it's a coworker; her husband spends time nowhere else. When they're introduced, she doesn't catch the other woman's name—it emerges from Liam's mouth half-chewed. Still, she senses some weight in the name, in the lilt his throat makes: she's a thing that has lived in him for a long time.

The other woman wears a red lip, and not a trace remains on her teeth, nor on the rim of her glass. The other woman is leggy and prim, in high heels so sharp they look like they'll dig right into the floor. The other woman maintains perfect posture, seated across the hall in conversation with several other men her husband's age. The other woman is alabaster—if set down too firmly, she'd shatter. The other woman has had two kids, and you'd never know it, the way her dress hugs her stomach like a second skin.

She and the other woman only crossed paths once, but she caught a whiff of perfume, in passing, and she spends the rest of the evening with the memory of the scent.

Back in the car, Liam says, You all right? Was it that bad?

In the flickering fluorescent parking garage light, the muddy yellow, his eyes are jaundiced, ghastly. That bad, she wants to say, with half her heart ripped from her, left on the restaurant floor? That bad?

C'mon, he says, and sets a hand on her knee. He gives a convivial squeeze, as if to a dejected friend, a downbeat sister. Look alive, he says, look alive.

He stops at a gas station on the way home to fill his car, and for a pack of mini donuts. You want anything? he asks.

She shakes her head, watches him depart. Her phone, she notices, is low on battery, and she opens his center console to find a charger. Beneath a stack of CDs, she finds a small box, gift-wrapped, its tag labeled with letters that are not her own. *MC*. She drops the box back inside like it's burned her, slams the console, leaves her phone to die.

On the way home, he munches on his donuts. Are you all right? he asks.

What do you mean? she asks.

The past couple days, he says. You've been a bit...ghostly.

So he can see her emptiness after all. Her curling around the wounds, her sheltering in place.

She hums. I'm all right, she says.

He grabs another donut, holds the package toward her. She takes one, splits it in two, sets half on her tongue. The fake chocolate leaves a thin film around her mouth. Crumbs fall onto her skirt.

She finds herself doing things without planning them. She opens her eyes to find the light falling differently, to find herself in a new location, a new room in the house, a new building. She opens her eyes to find herself in her car, parked at the side of the road, on her way home from work, tail-lights passing her in a steady red stream. She opens her eyes to find herself in a beauty shop, standing before a long wall of perfumes. Giant portraits of airbrushed faces and exotic flowers line the walls, foregrounded with bold fonts.

Can I help you find something? an aproned employee asks—A short man, nearly a boy still, with his hair in a ponytail, a swatch of acne across his forehead.

Maybe, she says. I'm looking for something…and she goes on to describe the scent as it has stayed with her, in all its complications—*warm light floral sweet delicious citrusy full delicate*. All the things that contradict her empty smell.

The employee seems overwhelmed by the barrage of information, out of his depth in the perfume department, but he clears his throat, says, You might like this one, it's one of our most popular. He steps over to a sample bottle, next to a portrait of a model—she can never remember their names, and neither can her husband— and spritzes it on a test strip, holds it out. And of course, of *course*, it's exactly right—the other woman is here with them; the lights overhead flicker a moment, as if her spirit has passed through the room.

It's perfect, she says, brushing the employee's arm with her fingertips. He reddens a bit, guides her toward the registers.

The small box, as she carries it out to the car, is weighty. In the car, she opens and unpacks it—the bottle itself is small, but the lid is solid and heavy. She spritzes a wrist, kisses it to her other, dabs it at her clavicle. Leaves the car windows down as she drives home so the city blocks are trailed with the scent of her, the fullness of that scent.

She walks into the house and finds Calvin strewn across the couch, tucked into one of her blankets, eyelids heavy, like he was just asleep.

Well, hello, she says to his amorphous form.

He makes a brief nod in her direction. Did he not tell you? he asks.

Apparently not, she says. But I saw your rental car at the curb. Are you staying with us?

Don't sound so thrilled, he said. But the chick I was staying with decided she's done with me. And honestly, good riddance.

Really? she asks.

No, he says with a sigh. Absolutely not. She was great. One of the best things.

She heaves her bag on the counter, pulls out her new perfume, sets it to the side. The thrill hasn't lasted—again, she feels empty. She takes out her dirty Tupperware from lunch, sets it in the sink, turns the faucet on to soak it, squeezes a dollop of soap in, watches it foam up.

Sorry that this is a surprise, he says. Thought Liam would've told you.

Me too, she says. Figures, though, he's fucking someone else.

She hadn't meant to say it.

He sits up suddenly. The couch squeaks against his elbows.

Wait, he says—what? Seriously?

For a second she considers playing it off as a joke, but her throat clogs and her face goes hot—she is in too deep. She really hadn't meant to say it, but the words had come pouring out anyway, and they'd torn a hole in the fabric of the room. The waning light is sharper now, it bounces off his eyes, which have pooled with fear, some shade of it.

Are you sure? he asks.

I'm sure, she says. But the question surprises her, so she asks, Why?

I just can't believe it, he says, shifting onto his side. He's so in love, he says. Like, *so* in love. Like, I've never seen him like this with anyone before. And I've seen him in a *lot* of relationships. Well—not that many—not in a bad way—you know what I mean, just, you know. Normal life stuff. He chews on a fingernail. But he'd better not be fucking cheating, he continues.

He takes a long pause. A moment of uproar from the golf game on the TV, then a return to quiet—no wonder he'd fallen asleep. He takes her in on the whole, properly this time. She feels his eyes travel the length of her, the way an old friend would after years of separation.

What? she asks.

You know, he says, you seem different lately. He eyes the red lip, the trim, the outfit.

I'm adventuring, she says.

It is adventure, in a sense. The tooth-wide smiles, the perfume, the skirting fingertips—it's a venture outside the costume of herself. Prodding those newfound emptinesses, finding new ways to fill them.

And I've never felt more myself, she says.

Well, that's great, he says.

But really, she says, twisting the lid off her coffee cup and dumping its dredges into the sink as well. We're happy to have you anytime, she says. She lifts the sponge and wets it. We've got the guest bedroom, no one's been in it since—

Oh, don't do that, he says.

She stops, sets the sponge in the sink. Do what?

Carry on like you didn't just say what you just said.

She shuts the faucet off and smiles down at her dishes. Her right heel begins to ache; she pulls her boots off, decides to head upstairs to change out of the rest of her work clothes. Before she leaves the room, she smiles at him wryly, says, Watch me.

She finds herself at a shoe store, wandering the aisles. When she looks up from inside herself she's in the children's aisle, holding a pair of lavender-soled light-up sneakers. She flings them back onto the shelf, and they blink red and blue.

She heads to the heel section instead, eyes the rows, seeks a sharp heel, like the ones the other woman wore at the luncheon. The way they cup her feet, the fullness she feels—like a cradle, almost.

Great pick, the cashier says. She beams.

The next day, Calvin decides he's had enough of his hometown. He finds a cheap flight and Liam meets him for a late lunch before he departs. When Liam walks back into the house, autumn evening cold dusting his cheeks, he says, What's this I'm hearing about an affair?

Her eyes go wide and glassy. Huh? she says. She's in a dress, short and leggy, and she taps the toe of her heel against the edge of the floor.

Her phone lights up with a text from Calvin: *bye sis. don't be mad.*

At lunch, Liam says, Calv asked me if I was having an affair. What was that about? He peels off his coat, slings it across a hanger, tucks it back in the hall closet.

She says nothing, watches him in his simple routine. This, when she was young, was what she thought life could be, someday—finding someone to perform these simple routines with, hanging up coats, slipping out of shoes, settling into couches. Together, all of it together.

Where the hell, he asks, would he have gotten that from?

He carries his shoes in his left hand, their heels touching, their toes pointed toward the floor.

Well, she says, shuffling her hands together, you are, aren't you?

He's looking at her, he's been looking at her for a minute straight—she'd yearned for his eyes on her, for weeks, yearned to feel seen, but now he won't look away. She wishes to push his gaze elsewhere, feels it on her skin like an itch.

No, he says. No, not in the slightest. Why would you think that?

But the condoms, she says, throat gone dry. I found your receipt.

Jesus, he says, the flush in his face deepening—those were for Calv. He used my card that night, I told him to go have some fun.

But, she says, you hadn't seen him yet.

No, *you* hadn't seen him yet. I saw him when he got into town.

But you changed your phone passcode.

I just got my new phone through work. You know that. And changed it to match my debit PIN. Did you try my debit PIN?

She thinks she tried his debit PIN, in her flurry of other tries, but she can't be sure anymore. Her head spins, like the world has shifted one degree off its axis—everything is the same, but balanced differently. She doesn't mention the panties, doesn't mention the gift she found stowed away in his pocket—she has these pieces, she knows she does, but she can't seem to access them.

There is no other woman, *mi cara*, he says. There's only you, there's only ever been you.

She believes him, she believes him. The belief is a balloon in her stomach, expanding, filling her. She understands: he is speaking to *her*, the other woman. She has lost herself completely.

No—she has become.

I love you, he says, and I don't want to fight.

And I love *you*, she says.

And is it not love, she thinks, to say I would relinquish every bit of myself to you, for you? Is it not love to have killed for you? Because I have killed her, the wife, the bitch, the broad, the wench, the crutch that clung to your coattails—I have killed her, and now you can have me, now you can have what you want.

But these thoughts stay curled in her throat because his eyes have glazed over, with that warm-watered lust, and his tongue has found her top lip, a flicker, an inquisition, and with her teeth, she reaches out, grips, answers.

ALL FADING NOW

I have never seen her like this. She's twenty-something, young enough to be my kid, and normally dignified, professional—always wears long dark pants and flowing tops, thick sweaters, bracelets I can hear clanging as she walks to and from her townhouse. Today she sits on the steps that rise to her door, her face between her knees, her shoulders heaving, and when she raises her head and sees me, she wipes her face and waves me over. Her bag and car keys have fallen to her side; her teeth are bared in a grimace that is almost a smile. She looks at me like I am a life preserver, though we have seldom spoken; she keeps to herself, normally, so I keep to myself too, smile at her when I pass her on walks around the neighborhood, feed my birds, sweep my patio, water my outdoor planters. She cannot control her breaths now; they come in frantic spasms.

Looking at her, I feel, for the first time in a long time, a desire to turn and run, to lock myself in the house and never emerge. I wish for the comfort of that, the security. But something else kicks in and I set my groceries down on the sidewalk, rush to her side. In the afternoon heat, she reeks of sweat, but she grabs my hand, pulls me into her, and I let her. I sink down to the stairs, allow her to sob into my clavicle.

Kristin—are you OK? I ask. A stupid question. I stroke her hair—it's been a while since my son has been home, and the gesture, the act of mothering, brings me a nostalgic relief.

She tries to speak, but her sobs are still coming too hard, so I prop her up and guide her through some counting and breathing exercises. I notice as I sit up that I am crying too. I wipe my cheeks with the sides of my fingers.

Match the speed of my breaths, I say, yes, just like that, a big, long inhale—feel all that air in your lungs. Now let it out—good, that's good. Count by sevens—let's get all the way to a hundred. Seven, fourteen, twenty-one, twenty-eight—good, keep going. Eighty-four, ninety-one, ninety-eight. Good, good work.

We sit side by side in a moment of quiet, listen to our breaths, the rumbles of cars on the faraway cross street. I think of my groceries in the sun, the ice cream turning to mush. Yet I leave them, turn my head toward Kristin. She needs someone—a body, an ear—and I am here.

I can't stop thinking about it, she finally says. Can't…can't stop seeing it.

Seeing what? I ask.

She looks at me, and something seems to pass across her eyes: some apparition, some other world. Then she crumbles again, guides herself back to my shoulder.

Once more, I calm her down, ride the wave of her emotion till she is calm and quiet. I run my groceries inside, put my perishables in the freezer, and return to her. She guides me into her house. It is strange to suddenly be this close to her, to be granted access—I have imagined her house in my newfound aloneness, imagined how she filled out the same floor plan. The place is not too different from mine, but her tastes are more modern. Her townhouse catches the sun's rays in all its mirrors and glass.

A photo of what appears to be her family is propped on the end table; she looks younger in it, around sixteen, unsure of her clothing and posture. What a lovely house, I say, and take a seat in a soft, up-holstered chair. She thanks me, puts water on to boil. Fetches two mugs from the cabinet, asks me if I'm OK with chamomile. Sounds wonderful, I say.

And it is wonderful—to be in a room with another person, to lock eyes with someone other than yourself. It's easy to forget that I'm over twice her age, that I could be her mother.

My son, Harry, has been urging me in his twice-per-month phone calls to get a pet to keep me company; he's concerned that I'm getting lonely now, tries to figure out what might help. I think, I was lonely even before. I say, What might also help is you visiting your mother. Which sends him off on a spiel—on the other side of the country, long hours, travel expenses—though I'm joking, I'm only joking.

Kristin brings the tea to the living room and sits on the sofa across from me. She takes a sip, stirs a pinch of sugar in with a spoon, then says, I saw a crash.

A crash? I say.

A van, overturned. On the highway. Watched it flip over. It... there was so much glass. Like hail.

She is neutral, narrating this now like she is orating a police report. Briefly, she shivers, then sinks back into her numbness.

I was behind it on the road, she continues. There was a pair of headlights further up, on the wrong side, on our side. Two-lane highway, most dangerous thing in the world. The van had just passed me, it was going seventy, eighty miles an hour. Didn't see the headlights, apparently. Didn't do anything. Just...hit what was coming.

I grimace, take a sip of my tea.

It went up in the air, she said, voice still void of affect. Like it'd been lofted up—it flipped, landed on its top. I can't stop seeing it, can't stop seeing the burst of it, can't unhear the slam of the metal—and I was in front of the van originally, I was headed for it. It should've been me.

No, no, I say, don't think that way. I take her wrist in my hand. Everything is meant to happen exactly as it does, I continue—there's nothing you did wrong.

I think, again, of Harry—Kristin reminds me of him. Taking blame for things that are out of his control, utterly fixed on his faults. Needing someone to be there for him, needing. I itch at my forearm.

She lets out a hollow laugh. I guess you're right, she says.

I don't feel convinced. Are you sure you're all right? I ask. Is there anyone you can call, any family?

I think of Harry calling me. Wish I had always answered, always.

I feel fine, she says. Weirdly empty, like I've gotten it all out. And no. They're gone.

I'm sorry, I say, and release her wrist. I think of my own absences, feel them warming my hands, my chest, push them down again, again.

All at once, she says. Car accident, if you can believe. I stayed home because of a test I had to study for.

Gosh, I say. My hands are slick, pressed together.

They were taking my sister to a volleyball tournament. Her team came in second. I never got to congratulate her.

I make some nonplussed noise, stunned, still, by the impersonality of her voice, the absence of feeling in her. Like these events happened on a TV show she watched years ago and has nearly forgotten, like she's struggling to dredge them up from where they have rested all this time. Like they're not fresh in every inch of her blood—but she's numbed, now, after letting everything out on the steps. Her body has expelled all the feeling; now she is blank again.

But enough about me, she says. How are you? You seem well, from my eyes.

I take another sip of my tea, swirl its bitter on my tongue. I think about how the grief has stabilized within me, but how it occasionally ruptures me. How my various failures have ruptured me.

I am mostly well, I say.

Mostly?

I focus on her brow, watch it twitch. I count the slight creases in her forehead, feel something happening in me, some remembering, some unfurling.

My husband passed recently, I say.

Oh, god, I'm sorry, she says. I wondered why I hadn't seen him in a while. She watches me sit here and darken. You don't have to talk about it, she says.

No, I say, it's OK, it's only the truth.

Her brow continues to twitch, like it's trying to inch itself off her head.

Losing him, I continue, wasn't easy, you're right. I feel it every minute. But eventually the feeling becomes less like the floor falling out from under you and more like a tap on the shoulder. A little reminder, a little thing, like: Hey, he used to do this one thing that you liked when you came back from getting the mail. He hated fennel and now you eat it all the time. Not the devastating way the reminders used to be, but there still.

She has set her hand atop mine now. Her fingertips are cold.

She says, in her flat affect, You saved me today, though she doesn't seem saved: eyes glazed over, like there is a film behind her lids she can't stop watching, the corners of her mouth barely raised in a smile, her voice never rising above its middling pitch. She has wrestled something down, and I am waiting for it to resurface. I am intimately familiar with the way the unwieldy things rise and fall, rise and fall, like they are floating on a sea.

In the evening, I imagine what it would be like to have a cat perched at the foot of the bed, limbs curled under itself, eyes squished shut in sleep. Purring when I scratched behind its ears. In the morning, I will call Harry and tell him that some parts of the idea sound nice, that maybe I am coming around to it. I will call Harry, and if he doesn't answer, I will text.

I fall asleep thinking of this, and wake when I hear a scream from the other side of the wall. From Kristin's side: a ghastly sound, seconds long. Then pounding on the wall: her fists, again and again, tremoring through the frames I have hung, causing them to shift and rattle.

I stand in my thin nightgown, pull on a sweater and some slippers, and tear out my front door, around the bend, up onto her porch. I knock, knock, eventually pull open the screen and go for the knob, but the door doesn't budge. The light is on, the single bulb casting the stoop in amber.

Kristin! I yell.

The door twists open suddenly, and she is there, eyes pooled with grief. Again she can hardly speak, but she chokes out, It was supposed to be me.

No, it wasn't, I say. It wasn't supposed to be you, you were saved.

I wasn't supposed to be, she says. It was Mom and Dad and Sara trying to get me back—

No, I say, they saved you, they saved you.

And seven people died. Because of that. It was supposed to be me.

No, I say, no, no, no, again and again, because I don't know what else to say.

The room behind her is dark, moonlit in patches. She turns to look at nothing. Eventually she hears me, says, You're right, I'll be OK, I just had a night terror, it's all fading now. She ushers me away, sends me back to bed, wears her best smile as I turn and descend her steps. I chew on whether to leave her be, but decide to follow her orders.

Halfway to my house, I turn back and give her place a once-over. I spot her in the window of her narrow third-story attic, looking at me with placid eyes. She throws the window open, still mutters to herself. *It was supposed to be me*, again and again.

Don't you dare, I yell.

I imagine someone else perched there—think of all the times I was not there to save him, all the times I let him fend for himself. All the times he needed me to talk him down. Of course he left this little city—why wouldn't he have? I run back to her porch, try her door, find it locked still—I can kick it in, if I need to. I dart back down the steps, peer up at her.

It was supposed to be me, she yells.

Don't you dare jump, Harry, I shout. I shake my head, shake him out of my eyes.

His voice, phone-tinny, clogs in my ears: *You weren't there.*

I'm here, I shout up to Kristin—I'm here.

She leans out the window, swings a foot over the sill, looks all the way down.

SMOOTHING

When she wakes, her fiancé has lost his mouth. He's still asleep, breathing through his nose; she lies curled against his side, skims his face with her fingers, ginger as a bird skirting the surface of a pond. Night-after-argument standard: they sidle back up to each other through touch, sugar each other up enough to skim through a talk. She remembers saying, the night before, *I don't care what you have to say*. His sweaty skin carries that alcohol-rancid smell.

Normally, she leads her hand down his nose, skims his philtrum, traces the curve of his bottom lip, spends a while there. This morning the moves feel false, gestural—there is nothing, no love in her touch. She remembers him saying, *I'll just leave*. Then she reaches the top lip, or the space where the top lip should be: her fingers flounder at the blank landscape like she is trying to find her keys in a dark room. His eyes flip open—his face has gone a frigid tint. He hates, she knows, to breathe through his nose: he feels fenced in, develops an itch all over. He sits, raises his hands to his face, leaps up to lean over the sink, peer in the mirror. All that space beneath his nose, screaming for a feature. The light has left his eyes.

When he proposed a month ago, she took his face into her hands and kissed his mouth. The brightest yes she could think. She thought it was a given, hadn't noticed his breath held tight, his wait for the heft of the word. Now he runs his wedding-banded hand down the left side of his jaw like he's feeling the skin for a seam, like he can unstitch himself. The night before had been the kind only sleep can erase, and, even then, traces remain in the morning. Nothing broken, some things thrown. Tears and saliva and sweat soaked into the sheets and pillows. Wine-stained glasses in the sink, an empty bottle washed out at its side. Clothes strewn across the floor, a rip in a new shirt. Her least favorite thing to be called, glowing on her skin still. His, hurled again and again in return. She remembers saying, *Everyone asks me why we're still together, and I don't know what to tell them.* The kind of night that touch alone will not fix—the kind that has left her cold, phoned-in, forgiveless.

Across the kitchen table, he holds out his hands, and after a moment's hesitation, she sets hers atop. His fingers curl around; his thumbs stroke slow circles. His limbs, stretched over the tabletop, appear thinner. She remembers him saying, *You know what, maybe it is for the best.* She has an idea: she leaps up, pokes around in the hall closet. She brings back a whiteboard from her classroom supply stockpile, remnants of old elementary math problems sunk into the melamine. She scrubs it clean with an eraser, hands it to him with a pen. Write what you're thinking on it, she says.

He uncaps the pen. She expects something elaborate, lengthy, overgenerous—the usual when he knows things have gone too far. Instead, he writes one word, holds it up like he's in a mugshot: HUNGRY. His face is sunken, sallow, beneath the single bulb that hovers over them. The board comes clattering to the table.

You're hungry? she says flatly.

He nods, gaunting, it seems, by the second, the cords in his neck pronounced, the flesh pared away. Fear pools in his eyes.

Anything to add?

He rights the board, lifts the pen, but struggles to steady it: the marks across the board are jagged, haphazard. He releases a whoosh of air through his nose, a frustrated sound; water wells in his eyes, spills over. The marker falls from his hand, rolls to the rug, leaves a streak of blue in its wake.

He stumbles to the car, increasingly muscleless, and she buckles him into the seat, floors it to the hospital. His arms and legs are thinning, minute by minute—his shirt dangles from him like it's on a hanger. She remembers saying, *I'm not listening*, plugging her ears, releasing a string of la-la-la's, like a child. The way he pried her fingers out of her ears—she feels his grip at her wrists, spots the bits of blue there now.

A red light stops them; she watches the procession of cars from the turn lanes. Almost there, she says to him. His eyes gleam.

In the hospital parking lot, she throws the car into park. She sprints into the building: how to explain the situation? Two women collect him from the car, wheel him in, lay him across a bed. He is so light, now—the nurses can lift him with ease. He's rushed away, and she sits in his empty room, waits.

On their first date, when his hair had still been short and she still wore heels, they'd met at a bar. Two cocktails on the menu leapt out at them, so they each ordered one and swapped halfway through. She'd laughed at even his dumb jokes—everything he said made her feel suspended in honey. It was a mini-grief when she never heard from him. But two weeks later, she ran into him at the grocer, perched over frozen fish: he'd been waiting for *her* to message; he'd thought about her every day. She'd shared this story at the engagement party—at the event's open bar, they'd offered those two cocktails only.

But this all feels to her, now, like a relic, something hardened within her, preserved in amber. Everyone will understand.

He's rushed back to the room: the surgeon tried to slice open a new mouth, but the wound sutured shut of its own accord, and his teeth, his oral cavity, have all shrunk away. The surgeon tried to insert a feeding tube, but the skin at his stomach narrowed, spit it back out. His legs have disappeared, bone digested whole within him, and his skull, it seems now, is shrinking: he seems nothing more than a fearful, deflating balloon, still with those big, shining eyes.

It might be time to say our goodbyes, the surgeon said to her alone as his eyes disappeared into his skull.

She is amazed by how quickly an ending can arrive. It has been coming for a while, but once before her, it loses its realness. She remembers him saying, *Oh, yeah, have a nice fucking life*. And she will. He has shrunk down to nothing: a cherry pit, a pea, a fleck of dead skin, glistening, in the harsh light, like an eye. What does she have to say, before it is all over?

PRETTY THINGS

From her desk Sophie says, Come here, Miranda, look at this.

I stand from my bed and wander over to her. She has just come back from a shower, and her damp-darkened hair smells of moringa. She gestures downward with her eyes: a bruise blooms on the ball of her left thumb, the color of mango flesh that has begun to rot. She winces as she prods it with the pad of a finger.

Ooh, I say. Where'd it come from?

No clue, she says, just noticed it.

Dark hairs have sprouted around it, near-black, much coarser and darker than what covers the rest of her arm. My face curls as I skim their ends with my finger. Wild, I say.

Sophie takes a piece of the thick hair between her fingers and plucks it out, holds it up; its droplet of follicle glistens in the amber lamplight. What the hell, she says.

Seems like there's something underneath, I say. The bruise is oval-shaped, protuberant.

Feels that way, she says.

It's kind of pretty, I say. Did you fall on it, bump into something?

Not that I remember, she says.

I'm tempted to ask about Tom, but I hold my tongue.

She carries on with her biology homework, studying slides of slick organisms on her computer screen, and every so often, she returns to the bruise. I'm tempted to ask her more about it, but I hold back, turn pages of a book, watch her from the corner of my vision. She prods it absently, rubs it with two fingers, cossets it in a curved palm.

Today is Sunday, which means tomorrow Sophie will disappear: since she has started dating Tom, she's spent less time in the dorm, become harder to trace, left messages unanswered for long hours. Lately she has returned on Sundays, run loads of laundry in the giant room on the ground floor, taken long showers, painted her toenails, read a few pages of a book. For the most part she doesn't talk to me, aside from the occasional greeting; she expends her energy during the week, uses Sundays to vegetate without my distraction. I step around her, turn the music in my earbuds down in case it leaks through, or in case she wants to talk to me.

When we first met, paired via random assignment, she treated me like a charity case, humored me by bringing me to parties, introducing me to her friends. I never got a good grip on her, always felt her floating through my fingers. Most of what I learned of her I picked up through eavesdrop, in the early or late hours of the day, pretending to be asleep while she spoke softly on the phone, of her new boyfriend, his age (25), her reluctance (more gestural than genuine). Things that sagged in my stomach to hear spoken to others—things she didn't trust me with, didn't find me worthy of knowing.

And it wasn't that I wanted, in the beginning, to be her best friend: I perceived, as anyone would, an immediate distance between us in the social hierarchy, felt the remnants of who we were as high schoolers shining through our skins. We were, and had always been, different girls—I understood myself as her marginalia. It wasn't that I wanted to *be* her either: didn't hate myself, wasn't itching for some other life, some other body. I just thought she'd learn to cross the social rift that existed between us; I thought she'd learn to like me, to see me as equal to her, as no less human. But it soon became clear I wouldn't get what I had hoped. I came home from classes, as autumn bled away, and found more and more of her things missing—her desk lamp, her good moisturizer, her navy jacket. Sophie had been thrown into my life, and she was now inching her way out of it.

I didn't like aloneness; I didn't like that it had chosen me, and I was tired of the way it had settled around me, coat-thick, strangely comfortable. And so I was bothered by her rejection of me, I maintained a cool front around her until I realized again that it was ridiculous, the thing I was doing, the fact that I had any expectations from her at all. But realizing that didn't make those expectations go away; it only reminded me of her rejection, reignited my loneliness.

Sophie comes back from the laundry room and empties her hamper onto her bed, sorts her clothes into piles. She moans, clutches herself: the bruise has begun to hurt, actively. She sits, cradles it in her hands, rocks with her elbows against her pajama-striped knees.

The pain, she says, comes in waves. It's like there's something in there, trying to get out. Do you have any Advil?

I do. I dig for it in my desk drawer, rifle through the old papers and office supplies that sit atop.

Two please, she says. She tosses them back without water, her straw-colored hair arcing over her shoulders.

Do you want to go to the health center? I ask. I am willing, no, eager to escort her; her strange ailment has become far more interesting than the chapters I've got to read by morning.

But perhaps my interest is too apparent, too dog-shiny in my eyes; Sophie looks back at her desk, issues a false Maybe. She sits and watches her wrist for longer, and her grimace recedes—her lips inch together across her teeth, eyes widen back to standard doe. Actually, she says, no—the pain's going away. I'll just keep an eye on it, I guess.

She folds her laundry, and when night comes, she gears up to sleep here for the first time in a month. She orders takeout, asks if I want anything, but my stomach is full and aching: I say no. Still, when she returns, she offers me a fry. I slip across the room, take it. It's gone cold and mushy, but the salt bursts across my tongue. When she's done, she brushes her teeth, settles in to sleep. Odd to hear the rustle of her sheets, her slight snores. I try not to speculate about why she's here, understand my tendency to lose myself in the lives of others, try to extricate myself from that fate here. Still, I can't help the notion that bubbles in my head, dizzies me like wine: she is here, she has chosen me, she wants to be my friend.

When I wake in the morning, she is already up, facing away from me, holding her hand out toward the windows. The soft blue light, raindrops clinging to the glass.

Miranda, she says, noticing I am awake. Come look.

I climb out of bed, slip into a sweatshirt, walk to her side. She straightens her elbow, extends her hand to me: the lump of bruise has moved toward her elbow and her thumb has disappeared; in its place, a larger one has sprouted, bony and pale, its nail square.

What in the world, I say.

It's Tom's, she says, it's Tom's thumb.

In her other hand, she holds a bit of shriveled something—blue, wrinkled like a shrimp. At its tip, mystified, I see a pink splatter of her nail polish. I want to reach out and touch it, but I am afraid, bewildered, slightly repulsed.

I try, in vain, to return to my reading, with class in two hours. I catch her holding the new thumb to her nose, her tongue, as if it might smell and taste different than the rest of her. I want to know what she's thinking; I want her to confide in me. She runs her nails, her fingertips, her teeth across it, as if Tom can feel it. The bruise-lump has moved up her arm, settled in the divot between her shoulder and neck.

She picks up her phone, smiles at it, sets it down, waits a few minutes; picks it up again, smiles at it. I hear her, later still, in the bathroom (my ear, yes, to the door frame): *Can you feel this? Where is your thumb now? I love it—a bit of you is with me always. You're giving me your pretty things and I'm giving you mine.*

She shows me a photo, just before she slips out the door for class: Tom's hand, her smooth, slender, hairless thumb attached to its side. She has slipped into wool mittens, says she'll claim a blood circulation issue till she and Tom figure out what is going on. She slides out the door river-quick, and it pulls itself shut it behind her.

Tom is a physics TA, with thick round glasses and a surprisingly plain face beneath. The glasses make his eyes into shiny swells, and when he takes them off his face becomes small and discerning. The sort of face, lean-nosed and thin-lipped, that I forget the second he leaves the room and remember intricately when I see him again. When I joked about this to Sophie, she wasn't amused. I have learned not to joke about him.

I blame him, of course, for the dissolution of my burgeoning friendship with Sophie. At first he came around a lot, before they decided, in some off-stage dialogue, that it was weird to have me around and preferred to spend time at his place. He liked to take his glasses off and massage the bridge of his nose with two fingers, like it was sore from holding up the weight of his analytic insight. He liked to look at my belongings like he was appraising the property, about to put everything up at an estate sale. From time to time, he asked me small, unimportant questions in some effort at inclusion, which made me feel worse, made me feel more alone.

Tom is dull, quiet; perhaps he unravels when I'm not around, sinks into some semblance of selfhood, perhaps there is something for Sophie to see in him. But he seemed so different, so unlike what I thought she'd look for—older, plainer. He eyed me, too, without any reluctance, held my gaze till I looked away, down at my hands, at the wall, till I swallowed, anxious. A deep-in-the-stomach feel: I had to leave, or wait for him to, before I could uncoil.

She comes in from class, slicks out of her rain jacket, and complains of an ache in her gums. Thanks me profusely for my Advil, which she continues to pilfer from; I've left the bottle at the corner of her desk shelf, so she can get to it without having to rifle through my drawers. She is objectively pretty, I understand, which means she is used to taking advantage of people without consequence. The bruise-lump is folded across her jaw now; she dabs concealer across it, though it still bulges, and complains of being too nauseated to eat, wishes aloud for applesauce, for yogurt. Falls asleep, snores softly, turned away from me, face toward the wall.

An hour later, she wakes choking. I watch her from my desk, raising my eyes from the essay I've started writing, in slight alarm; she rises and Heimlichs herself before I can stand to assist. On the third gut-punch, two small things fly from her mouth and strike the far wall, bounce off her desk, clatter against the thin-carpeted floor. Blood leaks from the corners of her mouth. She picks the bits up, brings them to me: teeth. And she smiles: two of Tom's small, square ones have sprouted in her mouth, like Chiclets between her sharp incisors. She runs her tongue along them, spits in the sink every now and again to clear the blood that still pools there, peers at them in the mirror, explores the diastema with a fingernail. Shakes her head, like she can't quite believe. Her eyes dart from the teeth to the mirror, never to me.

At night, she asks—awkwardly, with a mouth unused to its new-toothed configurations—if I want to watch a movie.

I brighten: Yes, I say, try not to seem too eager, too wag-tailed.

I join her on her bed, a few feet away from her, laptop set up between us. She scrolls through Netflix, and we settle on an old, vaguely problematic comedy.

The title card flashes on the screen, neon, block-lettered. The movie is about a sorority; the camera pans up a modest autumn street, houses branded with Greek letters. A frightened-looking girl climbs out of a Subaru, looks around at the houses like their windows are full of monsters. She is comically unpretty—we are meant to understand that this isn't the place for her, that it never will be. I resent the floating feeling I have at being included by Sophie, try to squash it down.

Fifty minutes in, Sophie stands to go to the bathroom, tells me I can leave the movie playing. The main character has just expelled beer from her nose and it drips like a leaky faucet. She stands on the lawn of a Greek house, wipes her nose, looks up and out at the world, wonders how she got here. Her makeup is comically overdone, clothes comically tight.

Sophie's phone lights up with a text while she's gone, from Tom. I lift her phone, eyeing the bathroom, making sure she is safely away. I read the message: *Can't wait to be back. Sorry you're stuck with the roomie. Still good to pick me up from the airport?*

Of course, I think, with a pit opening in my stomach. It isn't that she wants to hang out with me, but that she is out of options. Shame burns bright in my cheeks.

She pays no mind, of course, to my darkened mood when she returns, just slips by me and back into her spot, opens her phone, and types. Opens her phone every two minutes, types. When I laugh, she lets out a delayed, halfhearted sound, something like a laugh. Goes back to typing.

In the movie, the main character calls her best friend from back home, who doesn't pick up. Later, hooking up with someone in a dark upstairs bedroom, her phone lights up with a text that she doesn't see but that we, as the audience, are allowed to see, blown up on the left half of the screen, glowing against the wall in the black-dark of the bedroom: *y r u trying to be someone ur not?*

Heavy-handed, maybe, but it makes me feel something.

Sophie opens her phone, types.

Somehow, I made it through all of the university's throw-fresh-men-together events—movies on the sticky quad lawn, outdoor carnivals with red numbered raffle tickets, bus-route tours, classroom icebreakers—and emerged without a single new good friend. Nothing more than classmates texting to ask about homework, about due dates.

At my best moments I consider this a symptom of my pickiness; at my worst, it feels like a character defect, some blemish to scrutinize myself for: a blemish of mind, of spirit? Something externally legible, some waving red flag?

At my worst, I think of Sophie's repeated slights and Tom's insult, turn them over in my hands, allow a small swell of anger to form, to suppurate. She has remained off-radar since the movie, ignored my inquiries about her thumb, her teeth—whatever else she may have lost and grown— asking how she's hidden the teeth, which would be a harder task than hiding the thumb. She has drained my bottle of Advil and for some reason left it empty at the edge of the desk shelf. A shell develops, in the coming days, around the anger: to think of Sophie is to think of nothing, to feel nothing. I no longer want her as a friend, no longer want her company. I am proud, beaming at my ability to resolve a self-perpetuated problem. I spend a lot of time alone.

And it hurts, at night, to be left here. She doesn't come back to the dorm the following Sunday, doesn't reply to the inquisitive message I sent when I finally caved. Her textbooks, laid flat at the corner of her desk—the inessentials, I assume—acquire a layer of dust. My tube of toothpaste runs out, so I pull hers from her drawer and squeeze a strip out, leave the tube on the counter. The room fills with a heavy gray-orange, rainwater outside rushing downhill, into the gutters. I open the windows, let the sound in, let it fill the empty space.

*

The rain never lets up, streams steady down the roads, hangs gray overhead. On my way to class, through drops that accumulate on my phone screen, I squint to read her message: *wanna come over for dinner at Tom's tonight?*

I blink, close and reopen my phone, wait for the inevitable follow-up, that she sent the message to the wrong person, but it doesn't come. My chest twinges again with some weird hope. I understand how it is when people are in fresh relationships: they forget about the marginalia. I have been forgotten, yes, but now I am being remembered.

When the time comes, I almost request an Uber but decide, at the last minute, to walk the mile-and-a-half. The rain has slowed to a mist, temperature risen from cold to cool. Tom's apartment sits at the north end of campus near Greek Row. His entryway is tucked beneath a vine-covered arch; bulbs of soft orange light pour through his window. His bike is chained along an iron fence, a wooden bench stretched along the porch near the windows. I can see Sophie inside, the back of her ponytailed head, poking over the couch, her arm curled over its back, her face angled into the kitchen.

When I ring the doorbell, she stands and hobbles over to me. She pulls the door open: his foot has sprouted from her ankle, broader and longer than her own. Tom hobbles in from the kitchen, wearing two different shoes, one black and one pale brown: one of his, one of hers. Hi, they say together, then look at each other.

I shed my rain jacket, hang it in the entryway, join Sophie in the living room. Tom returns to the kitchen, rolling pasta, zesting a lemon, grating parmesan. Sophie's thumb, at the side of his hand, is pressed against the cheese block. Music streams from his tinny phone speakers.

He is different here, less appraising: he floats somehow, on his unsteady feet, around the space, chats with the two of us, still in his deep half-octave, though his tone has warmed. He asks me about my classes, my major, my friends, and for the first time, he sounds like he genuinely cares; he still maintains his strange eye contact, but today his tone is different, lightened, like he asks out of investment rather than obligation. A warmth spreads through me down into my stomach.

The TV behind me is paused in the middle of what looks like a reality show. A blonde woman, crouched in a beanbag, has her head in her hands; another woman, tall and in joggers, stands behind her, finger outpointed in accusation. Two men stand in the background, arms crossed, eyes weary at each other.

Do you watch it? Sophie asks. Oh, god, we love it.

We just started watching it last week, Tom adds, and we're already on the third season—completely ruined us.

The "we" is new to him, to them—they wear it in the whites of their eyes. He turns, plops ravioli into the pot. Sophie watches him as he cuts, drops, drains, dresses, tosses, her body angled toward me, her head turned toward him. She turns to ask me a question, her teeth touching the backs of Tom's teeth; turns back to look at him, half-attends to my answer: she can hardly look away from him for a minute.

Sophie and I move to the table when the food is ready. It's odd to me, their relationship: they seem to belong to such different groups. But I can't deny it, the way, in conversation, they twine in and out of each other's thoughts, float over and under; the way he looks at her, the way he looks at me. I start to understand the gravity of the situation, the bone-deep need she feels, the reason she leaves the dorm for days at a time, the reason she leaves messages unanswered. Their hands, one laid over the other at the corner of the table, knuckles aligned with knuckles, the slow concentric circles they draw on the skin with the other's thumb. He looks at me, and I feel my chest redden, wonder if either of them notice.

They uncork a bottle of red wine, refill through dinner, refill. On either end of the pasta, during it. I feel it in my head instantly—it lightens me, softens me. No longer am I trying to poke holes in the narrative, looking for dark parts: I am believing it, I am falling into it, the beauty of it, of them there, together, blurring into each other. I drink too quickly, perhaps, but Tom is eager with the offers of more. I laugh louder than ever; I feel the effulgence of myself inside me and think: Ah, yes, there she is.

I step onto their patio to look at the sky, a foolish idea this deep in the city, in the rain. What I see is gray, overlaid atop gray, and the occasional plane, blinking in and out. No amount of wine can make it look like a star. My head floats around as if unfastened from neck, bobs at my shoulder. So light it could drift away in a breeze.

Eventually I am seated on the bench, or maybe laid on my side, elbow awkward between two planks of wood, and Tom is there, looking down at me.

Whatcha doing? he asks.

Looking at stars, I say.

He laughs, a genuine, burbling sound, like honey in my ears. His face is pleasant in this half-light, inviting, almost, and I feel something I have not felt in a long time, something low in my stomach, something warm and tender.

I didn't mean it to be clever, I say.

Are you going to sleep out here, he says, or do you want to come back inside?

I look around at the ivy, the haze of early-morning fog. The orange light bulbs turn the ends of my hair wild.

Maybe I'll come inside, I say.

Tom opens the door, holds it, waits for me to slip beneath his arm, back into the heat.

Found her passed out on the bench, Tom says.

Silly goose, Sophie says.

I sink back into the couch, the warmth of it. The reality show is back on—the four people in the living room actively shouting at each other now, the boys trying to stay out of it, heads wormed backward as if in an attempt to withdraw them into their turtle shells.

Comfortable? Sophie says.

They sit on either side of me but they still look at each other, still I feel the current between them—I feel at the center of it. Me, part of this vast, swelling thing; me, wanted: it makes me feel something deep in my chest, some new growth there. The heater is on, rumbling soft in the walls, blowing air through the vents. I feel heavy in my eyelids.

I slip away again, wake in near-dark, stretched across the couch. The sky is beginning to lighten, and Tom is next to me. My hand is on his arm.

You were saying my name in your sleep, he says.

I redden, I'm sure, but it is dark, he will not notice. I pull my hand away, think of a way to say I have no idea how it got there.

She's asleep, he says, in the bedroom.

I can see it from the couch: down the hall, the door slivered open, moon streaming through. Answering the question I hadn't asked: had she heard, did she know. I think of what it is I want, what it is he wants. His eyes are warm with wanting, half-lit. The feeling dizzies me. Slowly, I return my hand to its previous spot on his arm, near the bones of his wrist. Just a moment, two moments, before I will get up and compose myself and walk home. This place feels like something I cannot come back from, some course of action I cannot reverse. Tom watches me leave; I feel his eyes on me as I round the corner, feel them all the way to the end of the block, feel heat on my neck.

I understand the appeal of him, at long last: his neutrality is a challenge, to sink into his flatness, look for ways to pull him out of it. It becomes a quest to split him apart, find his soft center of personality, reap the reward of it. When he laughed at my unintentional quip—I was so drunk, but I remember still—the sound sank into my marrow. It washed over me with the pleasure of something I worked hard for. It crops up sometimes, in my dark room: a sound, a laugh, where there is none, a spark of light in blackness. I hold it there, think of it when I come.

I arrange to meet them again, at the end of the week. At Tom's doorstep, I wait to be let in, twist my rings around and around my fingers. I try to steady my breath, try to play it cool: I don't want to let Sophie in on my secret, don't want her to know how I'm thrumming inside. I try to keep my eyes off Tom, the curves of his shoulders, the caverns behind his collarbones. He opens the door to me and I step in, wander around the living room, socked feet on dark wood.

His left ear is shriveling at the side of his face, withering like an old grape. You're going to have to speak up, he says, I really can't hear too well. With that smile, the real one that I had to work out of him, that sends waves of feeling through me.

Where's Sophie? I ask.

She's not here, he says, gone home for the weekend. He crowds the doorway, hand on the frame, thumb looped around the front. The house, the space of it, gapes around us; the fact of our alone-ness hangs in the air, shimmers.

It is strange to kiss him, to run my tongue along Sophie's teeth, to feel her thumb hooking my hair behind my ear. It is a reminder that I want him, but she wants him too—it lights jealousy in me, among the spires of lust. She doesn't want me around, that much is obvious, but I have found someone who does: and I am wanted, I am powerful. I am lost among the couch cushions and floor splits and pale bulblight, lost in the wanting. I stroke the wilted ear with a fingertip, ask, Does it hurt? It is blue, like it has held its breath for too long. It is still his, for now—she has not taken it from him yet. He shakes his head, pulls my hand from it, clasps it between his own. Runs his fingers along the moles that dot my arms.

I cling to details of him now: in the early days of his relationship with Sophie, I wanted her friendship so badly that I thought of him as the enemy, tuned him out, didn't learn him. Now I have lost myself in him, yet I feel like I do not know him.

He texts me sometimes, in the late hours, gives me express orders not to reply. Deletes what he sends immediately, doesn't want Sophie to see it on his phone. Dreamy things: where he wishes we were, what he wishes we were doing. I cling to these too, hold them in my vision as long as I can before I delete them from my phone, to be safe.

Sophie returns to the dorm on Sunday. Tells me, for a minute or two, about her weekend at home. I nod along absently—I have lost interest in her friendship. She does her laundry, paints her nails, turns pages in a book. Remote, predictable. I watch her for passive aggressions, for any sort of indication that she knows, because I know, I feel it so strongly, and therefore everyone must know, it must be obvious, must be as legible as newsprint on my face. She says nothing: turns the page, picks up her phone, types a message, sets it down.

His hairs are now prickling at the skin of my underarms; when Sophie leaves to shower, I will send him a photo, figure it safe, say, *you are happening to me too.* His T-shirt, stolen unknowingly, is shoved in the back of my closet; while she showers, I will pull it out, hold it to my face, slip my hand inside my waistband. I am wild, suddenly, I am uncontainable.

Tom ushers me over again on Tuesday, when Sophie is in Microbiology, pulls his shirt up from the bottom, gestures at patterning on the skin of his slender stomach, at his belt line. Spots, fine and constellated. Moles, he says.

What's the big deal? I say. Sophie's moles.

Sophie doesn't have moles, he says. They're yours, this is you.

I look up at him, and he looks at me. The weight, the gravity of the looking, like something is being born here, in real time. The thought of what could spiral away from this moment, of what else could emerge, from him, from either of us. For a moment I am afraid: the thing is happening to me too, and I don't know how far it will go, when it will stop, how much of myself I will lose to him. But he sniffs his hairs in my armpits, licks at them, guides my hand to his newfound moles, below them. Unfolds me like he is helpless to stop.

This is how things go for a while: we meet in secret, sneak around in their off-hours. When I see the two of them together, their relationship plays out in monochrome—I know, now, where his true feeling lies.

Then, on a Thursday, near midnight, I hear keys jingling at the door. I startle, thinking someone, drunk and stumbling, has approached the wrong door, figure they will wander away eventually. But the keys make contact, twist against metal. Sophie stands in the doorway, rain jacketed; she peels it off, lets it fall to the floor. She steps out of her mismatched boots, one after the other, and stands in a pair of striped socks, her dark leggings that, against the dark wall in my periphery, make her look like she ends at the bottom of the torso. My heart ratchets up and my mind races with possibilities: she found something that she wasn't supposed to see, some message or piece of clothing or scent I had left behind; he decided to leave her, said he found someone else.

You OK? I ask, attempting nonchalance.

I look up at her: her eyes are ringed in red.

Tom is dead, she says.

The words don't land at first—I flip the page in my book, finish the sentence. Then they register, slightly. What? I say, voice barren.

He grew a new heart, she says. Body rejected it.

She gives just the beats of the story, rote, like she has told them a thousand times by now. My stomach drops open.

Too late for a transplant, she says. Clutching at himself. Right on the kitchen floor.

My pulse thrums in my ears. She wanders to her desk, sinks into her chair.

I wonder if she suspects. But she doesn't look at me with hatred, with vengeance—rather she looks at me with a strange peace, the calmness of a frozen lake. I worry she is going to cry, and I will tense up, but she seems all cried out. She lays her head on the edge of her desk, feels the cool surface on her skin, breathes.

You can let it out, she says, it's OK.

What? I say.

I know all about it, she says.

I just watch her, watch her.

I know, Miranda, she says.

And she's right—there is something in me, some force attempting to break my own walls down. Something I hoped she hadn't paid notice to. Something behind my eyes, between my arms, pulsing like a vein.

You used to ask about him, she says, practically beg for me to bring him over.

She can't be right—she's exaggerating—but I don't challenge her.

I didn't want to invite you to dinner, she says, but he thought it was a good idea. As a peace offering, as a kindness.

I swallow down the lump in my throat.

You never left him alone when he was here, she says. You made him uncomfortable.

No, no, I would say if I could move my tongue, *he* didn't leave me alone, it was *him*.

You started to say his name in your sleep, she says. It creeped me out. I didn't ever tell him.

She raises her head now, looks me dead in the eyes. Just let it out, she says.

She wants a reaction, a confession, some sort of outburst, something, anything. I don't give her one: I stand, grab my rain jacket, walk out of the dorm. Around the bend as usual, along the gray brick walls that define this half of campus, under the gray sky. I walk till I am at Tom's—though it won't be his for much longer, it will be gutted and re-rented—but I walk around the property, look through all the windows, at the place I knew for such a short amount of time, the dark flooring and white walls, the thick cabinets and broad windows, a place that somehow already feels like returning home, filling me with that same color, the opposite of longing, because for once I knew what it was like to be wanted, I knew what it felt like to take.

I go back to the dorm, hours later, after I have cried myself out on Tom's fog-damp porch bench, replayed the brief tragedy of my month and walked the webs of streets, and I swing the door open to find Sophie is, of course, gone.

I said, Isn't it weird, and Tom said, What, and I said, To kiss someone else's hand that is really partly your hand, someone else's ear that's really your ear, someone else's teeth that are really your teeth, and he said, Every relationship is just a relationship with the self, everyone looks for some form of themself in their partner, this is an illuminating magic. He ran his finger down my jaw, gentle as a tongue. I keep thinking of that. I feel painfully alone, for the first time in months, but I have forgotten how it used to feel, the pain of it is fresh again.

Sophie returns, days later, sets an overnight bag atop her desk.

Where have you been, I say.

I'm sorry, she says. I shouldn't have spoken to you like that, it wasn't my place.

No, I say, you were right—even if he did grow another heart, *my* heart, I don't think he really meant it.

She just shakes her head, slow and sad, smiles like a hospice nurse. What? I say.

It wasn't your heart, she says.

What? I say again.

It wasn't your heart, she says again.

We can't really know, I say.

She just looks at me, says Miranda, oh, Miranda, slow and soft, like some great secret of the universe has been kept from me and I am just now learning it. And hasn't it, and aren't I? I thought she would look at me like we were together in this, like we had both loved and lost, but she looks at me like the sorority sisters looked at the girl in the movie, knocking on their doors, wanting to rush. She looks at me like I am finally understanding, after all these months, what sets us apart, what has always set us apart. The life that beauty has given her, measured against the life I will never have.

But things aren't quite the way she sees them, are they? I have something she doesn't realize—a power, an exigence. Making Tom shudder like a sheet in a breeze.

It wasn't yours either, I say.

She looks at me, still smiling that sad smile.

A thumb for a thumb, I say, a tooth for a tooth. This time was different.

Her smile drips from her, inch by inch, falls away.

Yours didn't change, I say, you're still here, still alive. And I am too. It was someone else.

She thinks, lowers her head into her hands. Stays that way for a while. I go to the bathroom and come back to find her still seated there. Just her breaths, the slow rise and fall of her back.

One of Tom's students makes a post on the university's Facebook page—an eighteen-year-old, as of last month, who, in her profile picture, stands at the top of a mountain, overlooks a densely forested valley, holds her clenched fists in the air. She smiles, wide and dimpled, in sunglasses. Her legs are tan—she looks vaguely like Sophie, in face and outline, if Sophie spent more time outdoors. The girl's post is widely liked and shared by the time I see it, and deleted so quickly afterward I wonder if it was real at all. But Sophie has screenshots, and we pore over them together till the words take root in my brain, till I exhaust myself trying to get them out. Not so different, the two of us, sitting there, staring at them. Both of us duped, both of us reeling.

have lost the love of my life today.
    Tom _____.
                        made me feel like no one else could
        . The last time I saw him
               even though he was my teacher I still
                              feels like the end of
   loved each other so much it was like
                    join him if I could.

There are more in the coming days: three more of his students, two girls and a boy, heartbroken, lost. Perhaps the heart that grew inside him was a wrangled amalgam of all five of ours, or perhaps it was none, perhaps it was another of his own.

Sophie still spends lots of time outside the dorm room, with her friends and occasional study groups, but there are things only I un-derstand, things she can confide in me alone. In this manner, we find we've reached a truce. Across all this time, all this space, with the prism of Tom in between us, we have come to learn each other in new ways—I look at her and see different versions of her, de-pending on how the light strikes. The parts of herself she held onto; the parts of her that burned up, where his light touched.

She holds a textbook open on her desk, tries to find normalcy in all this. The delicate bones of her wrist, still hers. The thumb that sprouts from its side, a piece of him. She frowns, with her thin brow. Smiles, bears his teeth. How to find the line, how to tell where she ends and he begins.

We have a disagreement about his personality. She says he was tender, funny; for me, he was purely a wanting thing. He filled the gaps of himself with what we he saw in us: he knew I wanted to be wanted, and so he wanted me. Simple as that.

I still think I feel his heart kicking around in me sometimes—I push the thought down, recognize my own rhythms. In time, his hairs fall out of my arms, his teeth from Sophie's mouth, his thumb from her hand, his ear from her head, his foot from her ankle. We grow back into ourselves. We renew.

BERGAMOT

They've cracked the code, they tell us. It's only a brief radio seg-ment, but it brings my Yaris to a pause at the side of the snowy road, puts a hitch in my breath. A near-crawl, fifteen miles an hour, given the inclement conditions—I've watched the flakes fall, ignored the wood-creak of my empty stomach, the itch in my skin. Two or three hours ago, I ate an orange, which is to say I peeled it apart over my office desk, split it segment by segment, laid them out atop a napkin, bisected each with my teeth, chewed each half fifteen times apiece, on either side of processing an invoice. My radio reception is poor, something to do with the antenna.

It can all be over, the crackling voice says. There's a website, an easy link, to find out more; a phone number to call for a consulta-tion. It's a glimmer of promise, moonlight over a rustling lake.

At home, I plug the site address into my laptop, scroll through. I don't care about the photos, the testimonials, the tape-measured waists, the grins: I want the science. The cure, they say, lies somewhere at the intersection of cortisol and ghrelin—it razes away at the receptors, scrubs them clean. A flood of leptin, of dopamine. As easy and neat as sleeping.

By the time Conor comes home, broad Irish face ruddied from his car heater, I've sent the studies to our office printer, brought the sixty-page pile to our coffee table, tucked myself beneath a blanket where I've pored over the statistics, checked for sample sizes, confounding variables, limitations. It's all clean, airtight. I can hardly believe it.

Conor kisses my forehead. My hard worker, he says. I thought you weren't bringing the office home anymore.

I'm not, I say. This isn't work.

He lifts a dubious brow, says, OK, Mik.

He heads toward the kitchen, passes through the hallway in which photos of his family hang. Not the tallest, but broad-shouldered, thick-boned; I watch his back as he moves, the dip in the middle beneath the shirt's tight fit. He can eat anything and it'll slick off him like water. Want a snack? he asks from the other room.

Redness settles in my cheeks. I turn the page, tuck the blanket further beneath my legs. There's a box in the trash—I'd flattened it, slid it all the way down, so he wouldn't see.

No thanks, I call. My stomach burbles, exposes its pleasant fullness. I turn back toward the sheets, the other studies they'd cited. There must be a missing link somewhere, a reach too far, an exposed piece of the machinery—I feel fated to find it.

Two weeks ago, he went dead soft. We've had more sex since, but he's seemed cloudy-eyed, removed, like his soul was halfway out of his body. He assured me the softening didn't mean anything, planted kisses at my shoulders, my clavicles, my breasts. Got me off, or at least tongued and touched me till I summoned a fake noise from somewhere in me, some half-dead part, and rolled over. It doesn't mean anything, he said; he blamed work fatigue, the hordes of students at his office hours lately, all the undergraduate theses he's chairing. I tried to smile through a lie but I've never been able. It doesn't mean anything, he repeated. His insistence, like a toddler standing over a broken dish, doubling down on his lie: *I didn't do it.* I slip the pile of studies, ream-thick, into my work bag—I don't want him to look. I'd rather let him believe that I'd lied, that I'd finally figured out how.

In the study kerfuffle, I'd forgotten about dinner. I don't cook for him every night—it's 2023—but tonight is one of my regularly scheduled nights. When the sunset's last blood streaks the sky, I leave the apartment, head to the store. I peer toward the far side of the frozen aisle, and my stomach leaps. How is it possible to recognize someone only by the way they walk, the hunch in their shoulders? And yet I do: I hold a hand out, stop Teagues as she rounds the su-permarket aisle. As she nears and grins big, I take her in—envy licks at me, pulls my mouth into a bruised smile. The stretch marks in her narrow arms, the looseness of her shoulders: the skin appears hand-stitched, composited by a kinder god. I ask her how the hell she is.

She proceeds to tell me—as I knew she would, somehow—about the company I heard on the radio. Twenty, she says, already. I can't believe it. It's been two weeks. And I'm down *twenty*.

That's great, I say, imagining a duck swimming atop a pond to keep my voice light, supportive. I move my handbasket to my other elbow. The top layer: oranges, parsley, a hunk of salmon, a cardboard tray of broccolini. All the prizes hidden underneath. In Teagues's basket, a loaf of bread, a couple jars of nut butter.

She says, I signed up for one of their last trials just before they went public. Gathering testimonials or whatever. Today's my first day back in the real world—haven't left the apartment in two weeks. It's smaller than our undergrad one, no shit. I'm sure Ben's about to start *another* podcast about living with a demon nonstop for two straight weeks. Lockdown wasn't even this bad. But anyway, it's so cool to run into *you*! You two should come over for dinner or some-thing·soon!

Teagues's eyes are bright as an infant's. She had devoted under-grad to her cause: she'd written research papers about body pos-itivity, published opinion pieces about advertisement campaigns, rallied for larger clothing sizes in the campus shops, spread flyers, held meetings, started petitions, megaphoned at curbsides.

My cravings, she continues, have just disappeared. It's like mag-ic, really. And no, they're not paying me to say that!

In the poetry class we took together, she'd written an ode to the Oreo: she performed it in front of the class on the last day for extra credit. The room had burst into applause, and the teacher had praised her for her adherence to a strict meter.

I think I want to try it, I say.

Are you serious? she asks. I don't know if you need to—you look great. Her words ring hollow, like she's reading them off a teleprompter at the far side of the aisle. I can't take my eyes off the blip of skin above her skirt—as she turns and rustles, her shirt lifts and falls, and it flickers in and out of view. I reach for my coat zipper, tug it tighter.

In the parking lot, after her taillights trail down the row and disap-pear, I revisit the website. I scroll through the clementine-colored testimonials, pay attention to them this time. The seventh girl on the page, beaming like an orange slice, with a tape measure wrapped around her waist: Jennifer Teagues, 31.

Conor and I have talked about it before, my lack of belief. One of our first real arguments, five months in: we sweated on his balcony, with sun-spoiled bowls of sorbet between us, melted to sludge. Un-seasonable heat that seeped through to our heads, too. I don't even remember what the fight was about: the first intense one is like that, it sprouts from nothing, takes on an unruly weight, and all we take away from it is the form, leaving the content behind. But his voice, both our voices, had risen to volumes I'd never heard before.

I said, OK, well, maybe I'll just leave. He said, Really, you're just gonna leave? I said, Yeah, I'll just leave. He said, Why are you just leaving, can we not talk through this? I said, It's not like you really want this anyway. My voice was needle-thin, and the balloon popped, the pressure fell away. His mouth moved, searched for the right vowel shapes, but no words would come. So he took a long shower, let his confusion and guilt rinse away. I stayed on the porch, watched the light bleed out, let my sweat turn to a crust.

When he'd dried off and dressed, he rejoined me, said: I can't believe you think that. Like, I genuinely can't wrap my head around it. He slumped in his seat in a way I'd never seen—he was always alight, upright, eager to leap up. He thought he'd done something wrong: done too little, maybe, not been earnest enough, let the pattern of our lives become rote, boneless. He went through elaborate efforts for a while after—complex surprises, restaurant reservations, flowers, concert tickets—but my perception of him, of us, did not change. He told me it was like trying to sway an empty room. He has spent four years on my side, never strayed. Still, I wait.

On the way to work every day, I pass a billboard with three girls in bathing suits at a waterpark: LOVE THE SKIN YOU'RE IN, it says in bold letters the color of watermelon flesh. The girls are mid-laugh, like the person behind the camera has just told a good joke. Sometimes, when the roads are snowed over or frozen slick, like this morning, I spend more time before the image. Often, I wonder how long till it's replaced with something else.

Every day it inspires a different feeling in me, a variation on a theme. Today I think of my mother, the way she hid me in the back of family photos behind thin-limbed siblings and cousins. My aunts, uncles, out of frame, when they thought I couldn't hear: What are you feeding her? The way my mother trained me, as we leaned over the sink and eyed the mirrored versions of ourselves: Chin up, never let your chin come down. See? When I lowered my chin, she poked at the pudge in my neck with a pointed nail, like she could pop it. The oink noises my cousins made at family gatherings, the pig noses an aggressive classmate drew on my homework as I handed it up the row: graded, returned to me with illustrations I hadn't made. Be nice, my grandparents said. I was grateful to my cousins, the row of them lined up before me: they had helped me disappear.

At work, I dropped the pile of studies onto the desk, and Kaley, in passing, nodded approvingly, as though I'd taken work home with me when really I hadn't thought about the office since clocking out the afternoon before, if not earlier. On the foam cubicle walls, I've pinned a few pictures of Conor, a couple studio portraits of my nephews. Last year, Conor said, An apartment can be just as homey as a house, we just have to imagine. He wanted to decorate, to personalize: he bought empty frames, tap-tapped small nails into the drywall, lined the frames neatly in the hall. For our family photos, he said. He sent prints off to Kinko's, filled his half quickly, like it was an art assignment due the following week. But I wanted none of my own hung up. I tried to pass it off as a joke: How funny would it be, I said, if we kept the stock families in the frames?

For about a week, he was chilly and impersonal as we ate, slept, watched TV: my irreverence, I assumed, had hurt him. When he asked again, the air fell from the sails of my resistance: Fine, I said, I'll hang some. I printed them, slid them into the frames, fastened their backs.

He spotted my additions when he came home from work. You're not in any of these, he bristled, like I'd made a game of his request.

Yes I am, I said, in the back.

He brought himself nearer to the photos, though I was perfectly visible from far away, tucked in the back, there, on the right. Wait, he said: that's you?

Yes, I said.

Where are the photos where you're in the front?

There aren't any.

He frowned in disbelief.

At all, I said. Go through my hard drive, ask my mother, I don't care, these are all there are.

I fled to the bathroom, washed my face. I avoid looking in mirrors whenever I can. I've changed over the years—lost weight, aged in the face—but in my head I'm the same girl, squished in among her family, cowering before the camera.

Conor's unique—generous, emotionally intelligent, considerate, able to multitask to a degree—but he's still a man. He collects his favorite porn in a Notes document on his iPad. He knows I know: he showed me, even. Every now and then, when he's not home, I go through it, learn some new tricks. Like a cheat code, taking the guesswork out of it. He likes point-of-view videos; he likes close-ups. I imagine him imagining himself into the scenes, driving himself into these women—with their faces cropped out, legs splayed and shaking, they could be anybody. On kinder days, I like to think he imagines me; one of them even has a mole on her back in a similar placement to mine.

A couple videos have been added since the last time I went through the doc. I thumb through them with interest, feel something in me begin to awaken till I skim through the montage I've assembled in my head, notice that all the video girls look like me—with my dark hair, my narrow nose, my skimmed-cream skin—but thinner, and everything in me goes back to sleep.

You're so beautiful, Conor says into the skin between my shoulder and neck, where his lips rest, and the words settle inside some false version of me, one reflected in certain light, not the version at my core. Yes, she's beautiful, I say in my head, the girl you see who exists in some separation from myself. I see it lying there in silence, a spread of flesh.

That silence is where truth comes in: even if the studies weren't empirically airtight, it wouldn't have taken much to convince me to try. The pills come a couple days later, in a mandarin-colored box with white writing: YOU CAN BE CLEAN AGAIN, they promise. I snap a picture of the box, send it to Teagues. *Lucky!* she shoots back instantly. *I can't find another box and my trial is over!!*

The capsules are red and white, little gelatin-shelled life preservers. As the instructions say, I toss two of them back with water, swallow. I keep the box at the bottom of my makeup drawer, where Conor never looks.

I'm lucky to have gotten a box, to have been early on the scene: the company can't produce the pills fast enough. Within days, they've infiltrated every major news network, disappeared from every supermarket shelf, exploded on every social media platform. Scrolling through Instagram, I'm bombarded with the mandarin-colored backdrop in ads and testimonials. Conspiracy videos pop up, twisting the cheery logo into something dark and muted, claiming the pills are microchipped, opiate-laced, addictive. Logo-stamped vans drive around town, orange-shirted employees behind the wheel. Passing the usual billboard this morning, I noticed crew members standing atop it, orange fabric gathered in their hands; they'd just begun to spread the image open as I passed. On the way home, I turned to view it from the other side of the road, spotlit from beneath: leaping girls with slim figures, orange smiles. That slice logo, like a grin. The cure is everywhere.

Have you heard about these? Conor asks in the evening, tone incredulous, when the ad comes on a streaming service. Our living room fills with its bergamot light.

Vaguely, I say. My next dose is due in a few hours—my stomach has become an invisible thing, insensate. The box says to maintain some low amount of caloric intake for energy, but I want to test the limits. Two pills, three times a day: easy enough to manage, easy enough to hide from him. Watching the ad models toss the pills back, swing tennis rackets, lob an orange ball back and forth, I think of telling him. But it's a decision, I ultimately reason, that has nothing to do with him. It's me, it's only me.

It's wild, he continues.

How so? There's something sharp in my tone, hard as I try to keep it out.

He pauses, parses carefully. We've, somehow, never spoken about my body explicitly, but he senses a delicate edge, crawls cautiously.

He finally says, Just the fact that people need these, I guess. He shifts himself around, settles a few inches further from me than before. Itches his socked foot, stretches it out in front of him, his calf muscle flexed, brick-solid.

There's a photo of him in the hall from early childhood: his skin hugged his ribs, his limbs tight as latex; his swim trunks dangled from him like they'd been strapped to a coat rack. In college, he bulked up, broadened. Sometimes, still, he forgets to eat: he goes weak and woozy, exclaims after a moment's pause, Oh, yeah, food. He's never craved in his life. I could defend the pills, the purpose they serve, and he'd listen, but I'm not sure he'd hear. In some ways I worry we'll never see each other.

A year or so prior, my undergrad friend, Murphy, called me up for coffee. Her name was Jen, but we'd had three other Jens in our apartment pod—Teagues included—so they'd each taken up their last names. This past year, she was going through a rough patch with her boyfriend and wanted to grovel about it in my direction—"catching up," as she'd call it. She stirred her white mocha with a wooden stick, licked the liquid off it. The sun beat down hot on us, but the wind that rose was cold; it rustled the shifting leaves, brought them floating down onto the outdoor tables.

She took a deep breath, readied herself for a confession, batted her woe-is-me lashes. She said, He watches porn. Like, a lot of it. I just found some of it on his laptop. And it bothered me, honestly. He said he watches it every single week. He was like, *I thought it was a given.* It's like, *I'm* your partner—am I not enough for you?

I sipped from my straw, got a mouthful of the sweet syrup at the bottom. It scrunched my face up.

Do you not wonder with Conor, she said, like, am I not enough for him?

The wind kept licking at my loose shirt; I tucked it beneath me so my skin would not show. I could feel it hugging my hip, revealing the bulge of flesh there. I couldn't decide which of my options was worse, decided to alternate between them. A moment later, the shirt again came untucked, flapped in the wind.

My answer leapt into my head then, a truth clear as if it had been written: *Of course I'm not enough.* I had a hard time voicing it—in my head it made sense, but in words it sounded ridiculous. My face wore my struggle plainly. Murphy nodded fervently, grabbed my hand across the table. See, she said—I knew you'd get it.

Conor kisses my temple in the morning, rises before me. I'm going to Target, he says valiantly. He makes a show of tucking his morning wood down into his boxers, putting his needs second, letting me stay tucked under the covers. He needs protein powder, tonic water, razor blades; I need sandwich bread, almond butter, makeup wipes. I've realized, after days on the pills, that carbs provide me the best energy, though my hunger has gone. He dresses, kisses my head again with minted breath, leaves me to sleep.

It's difficult to disguise my non-eating, especially when we're together: Conor is observant. My normal technique is to claim I already ate in the gaps of his coming and going, but to say I'll have a few bites of whatever he's made, whatever takeout he's picked up. This morning I anticipate something similar: if he offers to make breakfast, I'll tell him I ate while he was at the store. When I rise, I check my phone and find a message from Teagues: *still can't find any wtf?!?*

i thought you'd get free pills for life cuz of the trial, I reply. I leave my phone on the dresser, hear it ding with a message, but leave it for later. My pills go down easy today. I decide to sit in the yard with a sweatshirt and a book just to feel the sun on my face. It's warm for February, mid-fifties. The sweatshirt swallows me up.

The specific churn of Conor's engine approaches; the garage door rumbles on the other side of the building. After a few minutes, he joins me outside, sits in the other chair, says nothing. Birdsong floats over us. His eyes are up in the trees, the skittering there. Something is different about him in this moment, something slightly off-kilter.

I put your stuff away, he says. I'm gonna shower. He stands, steps back inside. It's easy to tell when something is wrong with him: he goes catlike in his hurting, crawls away to tend his wounds. I think, today is the day: he's realized, finally. He's no longer pretending—the four-year ruse is up.

I stand, sway, nearly fall onto the concrete. The last thing I ate: I can't remember. This, I realize with a rush of warmth, is what it's like: I can peel an orange, eat it piece by piece, and I can stop if I want to, leave the rest to rot, let the peel dry out, leave the segments to shrink up and harden. I can lie in the sun for hours, think of nothing. What a simple life this is.

The sliding glass door squeaks as I heave it open. In the kitchen, tucked into the counter corner, the oranges are piled in a bowl. On the island sits the box of pills, its contents laid out in a neat row. My stomach plummets. Of course: he put my makeup wipes away, of course he found them. He has counted the sheets, how many doses I've taken, how many I have left. The squeak of the shower handles from upstairs, the rush of water through the pipes.

He stands naked in the bathroom, runs his towel up and down his legs. I just wish you'd told me, he says. I lean against the door frame, watch him—he can hardly look at me. As he bends, the nodes of his back poke out through his skin; I want to trace them with my fingers, touch the fine down at his lower back.

I'm sorry, I say. My phone dings again from the bedroom, startles me.

I mean, he says, do you really think you need them?

A sudden rush: my mother. My chin, sharp, to blend the fat in. In every hall photo, my timid head poking out behind thin bony shoulders, long limbs. *Oink.* Conor's cock gone limp, shriveling out of me. *It doesn't.* The women in his videos, the juts of their hip bones, the folds of their clavicles. *Mean anything.* The girls on the billboard, the watermelon font. *What are you.* The orange-colored tennis balls, volleyed over a net again and again: this is what life looks like. *Feeding her.*

It's not about what I need, I say. It's about what I want. And I want them.

I am resolute. Conor raises his eyes to me, finally, takes me in. I peer around his shoulder, look into the mirror behind him—no one returns my gaze. Beside the door frame, just the light through our white curtains, wisps of furnace air causing them to tremor.

I exhale—finally, I am invisible.

I barely notice when the world goes white. When I open my eyes, I'm on the bathroom floor. Conor shouts questions at me, but the words blur together. Blood—nothing much, just a spot, but it's so stark against the tile, near-black on bone-white.

Look at me, he says over and over. Look at me. And I do, I'm trying to.

A former EMT, he wakes me, cleans me, tests my head. A slow trickle slips out of the gash at the base of my skull, fresh and tender. I've pissed myself too—he strips me, soaks that flash of acrid yellow off the floor with my shorts. He lathers bar soap over my skin, lowers the shower head, rinses me clean. All of this happens in near-silence, only the hissing of the stream, the occasional bell-sound of a text message. The air is full of scent, steam, unsaid conversation: ungiven questions, unreturned answers hover in his dark eyes, shimmer in the light over the bathroom sink, swirl around the drain. He lathers shampoo in my hair, massages my scalp with his fingertips.

Close your eyes, he says. I'm going to rinse.

On a date, early in our relationship, he whipped out his phone to take a photo, and I turned my head, ducked out of frame. We sat at an iron table outside a café, a handful of lilies stretching from a vase, tickling the glass of the café window. The sun was low over my shoulder. Behind his sunglasses, he recoiled like I'd reached out and stung him. I deflected, held a forkful of my clam linguine out to him, told him I didn't show up in photos. He scraped the bite off the fork with his teeth, chewed, sipped his water. You're the world's prettiest vampire, he said.

There has been a sharp increase in car accidents and fatalities this month, CNN reports, due to the pills. The subjects of the company's trials were all isolated: in the real world, people are forgetting to eat, passing out behind the wheel, drifting off the road, tumbling into ditches, scraping guardrails, peeling layers of metal off their cars like the skins of ripe fruit.

Conor tucks me into the couch, tosses a blanket over me, sets a sandwich and an orange at my side. He takes in the news, shakes his head. The air is thick with the potential energy of a large conversation, but neither of us steps up to take it. He goes to the grocery store for some saltines, my favorite thing to crunch on, sick or otherwise. Just rest, he says—we'll talk later.

There's a ricketing within me, like a kid stretching out in my chest, kicking at my skin.

It's nearly noon. I worry, for a moment, that Conor has confiscated the pills, trashed or flushed them, but they're still on the kitchen island, untouched. I gather the contents back in the box and bring them to the couch with me. I slit the foil of one dose, dump the pills into my hand; they lie flat in my palm like they're set on a scale. I hesitate, for some reason: they can't shrink me small enough.

Then there's a pounding at the door. I set the pills back in their wrapper, tuck it back into the box, slide it beneath the couch. I pull the door open to find Teagues, distraught, swaying on uneven feet, her eyes dark and swollen, her throat gaunt: I can count the nodules in her windpipe. Her silver Mazda is parked at the curb.

There you are, she says. Her scalp is slick, oily. For the first time in her presence, I feel a deep fear, struck like a bell.

Come in and eat something? I ask.

No, she says, I ate like an hour ago. I just didn't sleep very well. But listen. I'm out of pills. I just took my last ones yesterday and I can't find another box. Anywhere. Walmart, Target, CVS, Rite Aid, nothing. Even the old Long's on Broadside, which I'm pretty sure is the last surviving one in the country. I've been everywhere, and they're all out. And they're not even shipping them out anymore 'cause of supply issues. Where have you been? I've been calling.

I look back at the living room: dozens of potential answers swim around me. The news station has gone to commercial break— women doing yoga in a field lit orange by sun, the pill's brand name floating above the horizon.

Can I have some of yours? she asks, stepping into the room. You've got three weeks left, right? Can I have a couple days' worth, or maybe a week? Please?

Her eyes are gaunt: she looks at me like a life raft. She's sinking, sinking.

So I lie, in a panic: I'm sorry, I say, I'm out, I flushed the rest.

Bullshit, she spits. She laughs, as if it'll reset the mood, take back the intensity in her tone. You could sell them, she says, and probably pay off a car.

I don't dare take my eyes off her. I consider calling Conor. I think of his car, slowed by recent snow, crawling over inch-thick ice.

I know you've still got 'em, Mik, I know you do. She laughs as she says it, a lovely, earthless sound.

Come into the kitchen, let me make you a sandwich, I offer.

I'm really not hungry, she says sternly, I swear to god I ate like an hour ago, maybe two.

While I spread peanut butter on bread, she steps into the kitchen, opens a drawer, inspects its contents, slides it shut again. The whole thing plays out like a half-joke, with her lopsided smile: she moves on to the next, rifles through it, and so on.

Hey, I say, after she opens a fifth.

Hey what? she says. I know you have 'em.

There's a low hum at the base of my stomach, the sort of sense that indicates that this moment is unable to be perceived as real. These things are happening at the same moment, but they aren't merging in my head.

The wall hums as the garage door begins to lift. A sigh of relief leaves me, heavy, sob-like.

Where are they? Teagues asks. She digs beneath screwdrivers, tape measures, Sharpies, placemats, kitchen tools, utensils, scatters the drawers into disarray. Tools spill over the edge, clatter onto the floor: a screwdriver, an Allen wrench, an old flimsy steak knife.

Jesus, I say. What are you doing?

Where are they?

I bring the sandwich to her as the garage door opens—Jesus Christ, I say, eat this. She takes the sandwich, flings it behind her. It strikes the blinds along the glass doors, and they clap against each other, making that plastic rattle. The sandwich hits the floor, peanut butter streaked like shit across the tile.

What's going on? Conor says. He sets the grocery bag onto the counter, takes in the state of the room.

Where are they? Teagues turns her desperate dark eyes to him. He barely recognizes her, and when, a few seconds later, recognition hits, and he begins to assemble all the pieces—it's clear as day on his face, the procession of his thoughts—he recoils.

I think you should leave, he says.

Do you see yourself right now? I ask. You're fucking crazy!

No I'm not, she says: I'm *happy*. This is what happiness looks like. For the first time in my whole life.

My stomach flips. Is this, I wonder, what will happen to me, when I quit the pills?

You know what, she says to me, fuck you. She heads toward the living room. You've always just been there when you needed me.

And what are you doing right now? I shout.

Hey, Conor says, urging us toward calm.

She slides her mud-smeared shoes back on her feet, slams the door behind her.

I rip into the kitchen, tear the saltines box open, rip a sleeve apart at the seams, devour one cracker after another. I barely taste them: the salt lights up my tongue, and the crackers go down, coating my throat like drywall dust. I make it through a whole sleeve, two whole sleeves, like this. The roof of my mouth aches from salt, from the cracker's sharp edges ripping it open: it's tender, sore, as I prod it with my tongue.

Conor stands in the doorway. He has been there the whole time. He steps toward me, surveys the damage. You've never told me, he says. About this.

The sleeves are still laden with crumbs, with flecks of salt—I'm tempted to stick them to my fingers, lick them all up, lift the sleeve, ridged like an exoskeleton, and dump the crumbs into my open mouth.

You keep so much hidden, he says.

Why do you think you get to know every part of me?

He tries to reply but his throat is clogged.

I gather the sleeves in my hands, crush them together, let salt and crumbs spill over my hands, dot the countertop.

Finally he chokes out: I love you. Do I not get to know *any* part of you?

How to explain that my entire life has been an exercise in invisibility. How to explain it from beneath his gaze, which I can't escape. He sees me, he sees me. He says it to me: I see you. As I speak, his thumbs, gentle on my skin, wet lashes fluttering, eyes held to mine. Hours bleed away on that kitchen floor.

We flip on the TV, bleary-eyed, near the break of morning. A silver Mazda is on the news, wrapped around one of the billboard's poles, an embrace of metal and metal. They haven't yet identified the woman inside. The girls in the tangerine billboard image, mid-leap, appear to have bounced off her car and landed above the wreck. Shining down on all the passing cars, that mandarin-slice smile.

HEADACHE

There's a gift shop a few blocks west of my apartment in Wallingford, on the other side of the web of I-5. I pass the storefront on
my daily walks around the city—painted forest green, with a giant
white sign and a display, propped at the edge of the curb, with an
arrow pointed inside. Today, I decide to pop in before I catch the
bus up to my family's house in Lynnwood. It is just beginning to
mist, and a layer of condensation has formed on my rain jacket. A
bell sounds as I pass through the open double doors, and a woman
watches me wander through the offerings. She peers at me, confused, as if I'd wandered into the wrong store.

"Anything I can help you with?" she says as she approaches
from her corner.

"No," I say. "Just shopping for my brother's birthday today."

"Last minute, eh?" she says with a smile before clearing her
throat, realizing she may have caused offense. Her voice carries a
Canadian lilt. She hasn't yet figured out the polite-but-distant way

of this city. She tries again: "Looking for anything in particular?"

I glance around—at the wood shelves with mugs and chocolates and boxes of dried salmon, the walls lined with Washington maps and T-shirts and decorative towels, the counters crowded with water bottles and candles—and realize, with heat flushing at my neck, that I don't have the first clue what Thomas would want in here, what he'd be drawn to, what he'd revile. He's turning seventeen—what could he possibly want, I realize foolishly, from a gift shop of the state he's always lived in?

"No," I say, "just thought I'd pop in and look around."

I keep my eyes pointed at the ground, run my hand along my buzzcut as I walk out of the shop, hearing the bell ding.

On the way back to the apartment, I consider how slow business must be for the shop at this time of year and wish I'd bought something small. I think about turning and going back, think about how I'm showing up at the house empty-handed, wish I'd started looking for a gift earlier.

But I keep walking. Back at the apartment, I throw some of my things into an overnight bag and walk outside to the covered bus stop a few minutes before the scheduled stop. The ride home to Lynnwood is long—the mist has thickened to rain, and it drips down the windows as I climb on and take a seat. I should read my textbook for astronomy—my "easy" elective, with a surprisingly heavy work load—but I start thinking about Thomas.

About how, the last time I was at home for the winter holidays, he didn't leave the house the entire time, hadn't left it for a month and a half, hadn't even gone out to the yard. Mom delivered this news to me offhand, tried to brush by it and continue on to something else, but I stopped her, brought her back. He played video games, snuggled with the cat, ate meals at the table, but otherwise stayed cooped in his room. I took it all in, tried to reconcile it with the conception of Thomas I'd carried up to that point. He was an interesting guy, sure, and he loved video games, and he loved our mother, but he'd also loved his friends, loved the outdoors. I couldn't see him trapped up in his room and entirely happy.

But I was wrong. His childhood bedroom, which shared a wall with mine, was flooded with chip bags and cracker boxes, dirty T-shirts and strewn single socks, half-read books and used tissues. When he saw me, he beamed at me like I'd just given him a thousand dollars, tried to pull me in for a hug as if nothing was different.

I lost my shit.

By this point, I'd been living away from home for a year and a half, first in a dorm, then in an off-campus apartment with a couple of my best friends. I'd gotten used to taking care of myself, taking care of spaces, keeping them in check. To see Thomas clinging so tightly to Mom's care enraged me. I wasn't nice—I said my piece, stormed back downstairs, left my bags untouched at the top of the stairs, went to sit on the back porch. He knew me well enough by that point, I thought, knew I had to wander off and stew for a while, knew I'd be back to myself within the hour. My high school girlfriend, Lena, had made fun of my star placements, my double Aries—*It explains so much*, she said—and Thomas had laughed along.

In his room, I'd been livid, but later, listening as the rain plopped into puddles, I was worried I'd hurt his feelings. I gathered a handful of pebbles from one of the planters and tossed them, one by one, at his window at the back corner of the house. After a few of them made contact, tapped at the glass like tiny fingernails, his face appeared, sullen, stormy. I waved him outside, but he shook his head no.

Mom joined me outside on the other side of the stretch of porch covered by the awning, and said, "Things have gotten worse for him since you left. As you can tell." She paused, soaked in the humidity, then rushed to say, "Not that I'm saying it's your fault—it's not. It's just...you didn't know."

I didn't. When I left Lynnwood, went to my life further in the city, I shrugged off the house, the responsibilities of checking in. I felt a sort of shame, coming home and playing catch-up—it was like skipping a season of a TV show and listening to a friend shoddily explain it. But I couldn't figure out how to do things differently.

He'd entered into a fog after that first night and didn't quite leave it till I went back into the city for a new term of school. On Christmas morning, the three of us exchanged gifts on his bedroom floor—tidied, now, in the time since I'd gone off on him. He and I had gotten each other socks, as was our tradition, and he was bashful as he handed my gift to me. I removed the wrapping paper and found that all the pairs he'd gotten me were science-themed, animated with molecules and telescopes and beakers and lab goggles, a reference to my failed biochem major. He'd bought them as a joke, but the air was knocked out of him now. I handed his to him—plain black, as he preferred—and wished I'd thought to make a joke with them. I felt the socks as I sat there on his floor, squeezed them like stress balls.

It's a two-mile walk to the house from the Lynnwood stop, and normally I trek it, but today Mom offered to pick me up at the transit center. "Hi, Matt," she says; she pulls me into her shoulder, strokes the bags under my eyes with her thumbs, asks if I've been getting enough sleep. She too seems slow and tired—her eyes heavy, words soft—but I don't ask about it.

"How's Tommy?" I ask instead. A pet name he can't stand—I never call him by it to his face, only say it to Mom when he isn't around.

I watch her weigh things, watch her settle on "He's OK." She shifts into reverse, pulls out of the spot, adds, "He's excited to see you."

I wonder what things will be like this time, wonder how his room will be—if he'll have cleaned it in anticipation of my arrival. If things are bad today, I will try to contain myself. Easier said than done, but I can at least try.

"I made him a cake this morning," Mom says, slowing to a crawl before a stop sign. "Lemon buttermilk—you know he loves lemon. What did you get him?"

My neck goes red. I think of the gift shop, the rows and rows. Think of the other shops I could have gone to, the other things I could have looked for if I'd only started earlier. But I still wouldn't know what he would want. "I didn't really have time to get anything," I say.

"Ah," she says, falsely bright, trying to shine over her disappointment. A traffic light turns red—she slows, stops at the edge of the crosswalk. We sit in silence, punctuated every few seconds by the windshield wipers.

As we pass the strip mall by our house, the one we went to growing up, with the grocery store and the McDonald's, she asks if I want to stop in and get Thomas something somewhere. She seems strange, tense—I appreciate her offer, but I feel already like I've failed, like it's too late to make it up now.

"Let's just go home," I say, frustrated at nothing, frustrated at myself.

She asks about classes and I rant about them as we pass by the last few blocks, till we're parked in the driveway at the house and the engine has clicked off. I see Nub's head in the front window, his little ears perked up. Thomas is in the living room behind him, seated on the arm of the recliner, hair wet from a shower. When I enter the house and drop my bag at the door, he hugs me with reserve—something seems to be weighing on him. I take off my shoes at the door, revealing my socks with microscopes on them, but he doesn't notice.

It's only been three months, but he seems older, gaunter in the face, more hairs pricking at his lip. Still the same eyes he's always had, the same ones as mine.

"How have you been?" I ask. Mom has locked the car and come into the house; she digs through drawers, pulls out clanging kitchen tools.

"I've been OK," he says. He does a thing similar to what Mom did earlier when I asked how he was: he watches a film flash over his eyes of his recent experiences, weighs them against each other. I don't push him further, but perhaps he can tell I don't believe him.

"I've been thinking about the headache again," he says.

My stomach drops: when Mom had suggested his worsening

state, I was hoping it wasn't this flaring up again. "I don't know," he says, "I don't know." Shuffles his toes around in the carpet, looks at his hands, folded in his lap. "I just don't know. And I can't stop thinking about it. Oh: that reminds me." He walks over to the base of the steps, ascends them, skips every other stair. Pops into his room at the top, rummages around for something. I grab my bag to take it upstairs. Climb the steps, skip every other, as Thomas had.

Our great-grandfather died by way of headache in 1945. He was at work on the ENIAC in Philadelphia: The Giant Brain, they called it in the media. The first digital computer, capable of calculating artillery trajectories at a rate 2,400 times faster than a human. He was programming the machine and then he keeled over, moaned, reported a pain in his head like it was being squeezed in a giant metal fist. Then he was dead.

At thirteen, Thomas became obsessed with this fact. When I got home from a high school basketball game and found him sobbing on the couch, he explained it to me this way: *If it happened to our great-granddad, I just know it's going to happen to me. It was passed down. My head's just a ticking time bomb.*

His theory was further solidified when a year later, our father—who had started losing track of himself, drifting off in confusion, startling himself awake in the middle of the day, and experiencing headaches—went to the doctor and came home diagnosed with brain cancer. We buried him in the fall of my junior year. Thomas screamed in the graveyard, fell to his knees, felt responsible. He said he'd summoned it by thinking about the headache, said it was only a matter of time before he fell prey to it too.

His problem was he didn't know how to shove a thing down, to smother it. For a while the thought devoured him—he didn't want to put pressure on his body, didn't want to drink coffee or exert himself physically or stay up too late, lest a headache come on and put an end to him. He was worried when I applied to the computer science major, afraid I'd go the same route as our forefathers. I was hoping, when he stopped talking about it, that he left it behind him, that it was the end of things. But now it seems they're back, now it seems the thoughts are roaring in his head once again.

Halfway up the stairs, Mom stops me, pulls me into the kitchen. She's making Thomas's birthday dinner, frying chicken sausages on the stove, boiling water for tortellini. The pasta package is slit down the middle; she dumps its contents into the water. "I don't know why I didn't mention this in the car," she says, "but his friends...he hasn't really been seeing his friends."

"How come?" I ask. The sausages sizzle and spit—she nudges them with closed tongs.

"He says they've been making fun of him," she says. She turns the sausages, allowing the pale halves to brown. "Teasing him for the...headache stuff."

"God," I say. "Why didn't you tell me?"

Her eyes fall to the sausages; she pulls the cover over them, nudges the pan, stirs the tortellini. She doesn't look at me—her mouth is a tight line. Her hesitance comes through clearly: why *would* she tell me? She probably has tried to tell me, and I haven't answered her calls.

"All I'm trying to say is," she continues, "he could probably use your company right now."

"You don't have to guilt-trip me," I say. The starchy foam atop the boiling pasta is rising aggressively; she stirs it with her spoon, turns the heat down. "He's my brother. I get it."

"I'm not trying to guilt you," she says. "Just—letting you know."

"Great," I say. I leave the kitchen, walk out to the living room. Nub stands in the windowsill—I approach him, pat his head. "Hi, Nubby," I say. He looks particularly gray today—some days his gray shines through more, others his orange. He nestles his face into my hand. I rub his face once more, run my fingers down his back, then head upstairs.

I set my bag on my desk chair, look around my room. Most

of my things came with me to my apartment, but some furniture remains—the room now is an odd mix of the personal and the unfamiliar. My bed is still in its spot along the left wall, dressed in sheets I've never seen. The old desk and its chair are still by the door, lit by a new lamp.

Thomas meets me at the door with a box in his hands. "Don't want to forget this," he says.

"What is it?"

"It's for you." His eyes are pointed at the floor, but he wears a gentle smile. "Early birthday gift."

My birthday's not for another month, deeper into the spring, though I guess he's not certain when I'll be back. My hands suddenly feel so empty, my bag so light. "You didn't have to do that," I say, feeling regret churning in my stomach. He hands it over, and I run a finger along its gentle wrapping. "I got you something, too," I say quickly, "but I left it at home." I slip a finger under the wrapping, peel a corner of the tape upward. "Remembered as soon as I got on the bus."

"It's OK," he says. He won't make a fuss about it, I know he won't.

I peel the wrapping off, and inside is a square cardboard box. I pop its tab out, pull back the lid. Inside is a brass contraption—I pull it out, turn it over in my hands.

"It's a sextant," he says, "or a replica of one. 'Cause you said you were taking an astronomy class. It reminded me of you. Apparently sailors used these to navigate, measuring the stars or something."

He's always known to go for funny gifts, and I should laugh—the astronomy teacher sucks, and this will be a funny memory—but I feel, weirdly, like crying. I try to choke down whatever the thing is that has formed in my throat.

"I don't know if it actually works," he says, "but you could, like, put it on a shelf or something. It's cool-looking."

I look up at him. His eyes are wavering in the light—he's afraid I don't like it. I hope he can't see the uncontrolled emotion in mine.

"Thanks, dude," I say around the lump. "Thanks. It's great."

"Oh, good," he says.

"I need to—one sec, be right back," I say. A horrid swelling has started in my chest; I step into the bathroom, sit at the edge of the tub, set my head in my hands. I breathe faster and faster, try to slow it down. It's a ball in my ribs that is swelling outward, making everything feel tight—it's spreading to my limbs, a hot kind of panic.

It hurts to come home, to face my brother's goodness, his kindness; to see it contorted, twisted, in myself.

I splash cold water on my face then let the faucet run hot, washing my hands in the scalding stream. I open the bathroom door again, step into the light of the hall. When I get back to my room, he's gone—from his room down the hall, I hear his TV, the 8-bit music of a video game loading screen.

When I was home for winter break, on one of the last nights, Thomas met me at the threshold of the dining room. Trying to repair, I think, though I didn't see it at the time for what it was—my weeks at home were sullied by my initial rage-storm. I still hadn't apologized for what I'd said to him—I'd thought about it, recognized there was regret underneath the rage, but hadn't bitten. He'd shut down in the days afterward, and I decided that was where he was, where he'd stay, and didn't look for reasons otherwise.

Another thing I didn't understand then: that people changed their minds, or ever wanted to change them. That their emotional states could allow for anything other than a strict upholding of whatever anger-fueled decision had been made. I was stubborn in my convictions, and thus I thought everyone else was stubborn in theirs.

I was seated at the kitchen table, old math books spread all around me, tutoring websites pulled up in different tabs on my computer, graphing calculator uncovered and blinking. I took one of my earbuds out, paused the lecture video I was watching.

"Do you wanna play Smash Bros?" he asked, looking at the mess of open books around me, the chicken-scratch notes across my journal page. In the upcoming term I was taking Calculus III, and it had been a year since Calc II, even longer since Calc I: all the information had been sliding out of my brain in a steady stream since. I was grasping, I needed to get it back.

"Not right now," I told Thomas. I was stressed, I was myopic; I didn't notice that he'd needed me then, needed my company since Mom had gone to a friend's house for the evening. "Maybe later." I put my earbud back in, resumed the video, tried to follow along with the tutor's leaps in logic.

I remembered an hour later, too, that Mom had asked me to feed Nub: a treat, one of the cans in the pantry scooped out into his bowl atop the last few cereal-shapes of his morning kibble. The tab on top of the lid broke off when I tried to peel it back, and I couldn't find the can opener; I went up to Thomas's room to ask him if he knew where it was. It wasn't in the drawer by the sink, but maybe that's where it was located at my own apartment: everything was falling from me now.

When I reached his door, I looked in his room and didn't see him. The video game screen was still on, the remote set on his chair, but he wasn't anywhere. I almost turned to check his bathroom, but heard a noise from further inside, beyond his bed, a series of noises, of quick breaths. I pushed through his door, past his video-game station to the other side of his bed, the square space between the head of the bed and the corner of the room, where he sat, his spine curled against the wall, his head between his knees, his hands clasped at the back of his head.

"Thomas?" I said, lowering myself to his level, seating myself on his floor.

"It's happening," he said through his panting, each syllable punctuated by a hyperventilated breath. "The headache, it's happening."

"Stop it," I said, "no it's not. You're fine. Hey—look at me. Look up. You're fine." I didn't really know what else to say, didn't have the words to do anything other than bring him down to the present moment. His 8-bit video game music still blipped by in the background, replaying its same riff. His scraggly carpet beneath our feet, his dim lamplight. The fact that there was nothing more than this. "Everything's fine. You're fine. Your head is fine. It's all good. Nothing's happening."

He calmed, gradually—breath by breath, minute by minute. He was fine, his psychosomatic headache was going away, he was back in his chair, with the Nintendo remote in his hand, and then he was ushering me away, out of the room, back downstairs. "I'm fine," he said, "you don't have to deal with me anymore, I'm fine."

I should've thought more about it—should've told him it wasn't dealing with him, he wasn't something to deal with. He was my brother. But I didn't think about it; the crisis was over, things were fine. I asked him where the can opener was and he directed me, of course, to the drawer across from the sink, buried beneath some other tools. I hadn't looked closely enough the first time. I went downstairs, fed the cat, listened to his spiky little tongue lap at the pile of wet food, then went back to my math.

I think about staying in my room, reading my astronomy textbook and doing the reading quiz, but I pad up to Thomas's door instead. He notices my socks this time—smiles, brightens, though I can tell he's still slightly heavy, the thing is still on his mind.

"Wanna play Smash?" I ask.

He beams for a moment, then his expression falls. "You don't have to," he says, as if I thought he were a charity case, as if my question was a ruse.

"I know," I say. He doesn't move, doesn't say anything further, so I push past him, turn the system on, pull the controllers off the shelf. I sit at the edge of his bed, leave the chair for him. He takes it, lifts the remote.

We play a few rounds and I beast him, as is the usual. Every now and again, I hear him start to breathe quicker, start to fidget and overheat, and I say "Hey, it's OK." I bring him down, pull him back to the moment, as I had over Christmas break. I think of

Mom having done this for months now while I've been gone—the way I've ignored their calls, left my phone on Do Not Disturb in the name of making a new life for myself. The way I thought of my familial relationships as obligatory. How much damage I have done, how much damage I have left to undo.

Thomas turns to smack my knee when I beat him again after going easy for a few seconds. His head angles back toward the screen—from here, the bump at the top of his nose is pronounced, the bump he and I share, inherited from our dad. I think of when I fractured mine in high school on the trampoline and Thomas brought me ice all afternoon till Mom got home. He stood by me in the hospital when the doctor had to set it back in place and he didn't look away, he wanted to watch.

I don't know how to say what I'm feeling, but I know how to be here. I know how to try. I had to warm the muscles back up, remind them of their functions.

Mom calls up the stairs that dinner is almost ready.

"Wanna play some Kart now?" Thomas asks—he knows he's actually got a chance at that one.

"Sure," I say. "But I'll be right back."

I leave my remote at the edge of the bed, slip out into the hall, and he gets up to swap game cartridges. I hover at the top of the stairs, think of Mom helping him while I haven't been here, think of her talking him down from his escalations, cooking for him, sitting across the table from him, watching him struggle to maintain his grip on the world. Downstairs, she's gotten the chicken sausages sliced, I'm sure, mixed in with the tortellini. She's got the cake stand set at the edge of the counter, the lemon-yellow gleaming under the plastic dome.

Tonight I'll set the table, the plates and forks, the glasses. I'll ask Mom and Thomas what they want to drink. When we've eaten and the cake is shining at the edge of the counter, I'll bring it down to the table, pull the cover off, let Thomas choose his slice. I'll watch him take the first bite, watch his face scrunch with sweet-sour, watch him smile.

NIGHT SWIMMING

After a bad breakup, my sister moves back into the house. We pull her things from the car, me and her together, and lug it all up the stairs, set it on her floor. She left this room and fled to California in the heat of love—now the space smells like an abandoned thing, musty, stale. It's ninety degrees out, the sun sharp as a tack, but still she wears an olive sweater.

Be right back, she says: she paces the hall, steps into and out of the bathroom, flicks lights on and off. She has not looked at me once. I stand here, toes plunged in her spill-stained carpet, look around at the things I love—the brown desk with its sharp corners, the pushpin holes in the blue paint, the vine-like spirals of her head-board—and smile till my face aches.

She left the house three days before I started high school and now I'm about to start junior year. I expect her, after we unload the car, to hug me, assess me, compliment my makeup, the contour blending I watched her do a thousand times, practiced on my own till it was perfect. When I stand in her doorway, she looks beyond me.

I've got it, she says, with a bite like frigid wind when I reach into an open box and pull out some shirts.

So instead I pace around my room, straighten photo frames and windowsill succulents, tighten bulbs in the ceiling light. I want her to see what has changed since she left: the photos hung from wire string across the wall, the deep purple bedspread, the new knit rug, the candles lined on the dresser. Want her to see the girl emerging from these embers. I listen to her down the hall as she shuffles around the room, wait for her to call out, to ask for my help.

Eventually I crawl to her doorway, say, Can I just watch?

She gestures to her bed, which is still dressed in the same blue sheets as when she left, and I lie across it, chin nestled into my hands.

Why are you smiling so much? she asks. Her brows haven't lifted from their slant since she pulled into the driveway. Her eyes, the dim brown centers of them, are angled toward me. She pulls another box open and the tape screeches apart in her hands.

I missed you, Emily, I blurt. I feel myself sinking into an old skin, remembering who I was around her before she left: idolatrous, moon-eyed, brimming with questions. I want to resist this. I don't want to be the person she knows, the person she expects. The person she shrugged off like a coat.

She says nothing to that, or to anything else. I leave when she makes it clear she won't talk to me, won't say anything real. Back in my room, I imagine her imagining me: all the possible new layers of me, the complications. But I know she's not thinking of me—she's on the phone with a friend from high school. Been a while, hasn't it, she says, with a laugh.

The bathroom is once again crowded with her makeup and skincare, the shower with her bottles. I'd forgotten the way she filled out the space: everything, somehow, feels more real. I used to pilfer from her conditioner, a tiny glob at a time till she called me out on it. When my hair fell around my shoulders, it smelled like coconut, felt so soft.

When she came back from a high-school summer spent in Sicily, Mom appraised her: the deep tan in her skin, the light streaks in her hair, the bit of new weight at her hips. Dad and I sat at the table, bit back laughs as Mom pinched at Emily's extra flesh. It looks lovely on you, Mom said.

Stop it, Emily said, inching away from her. Which is to say, Emily has always shied away from affection—from Mom, from me, from anyone.

Mom gushed to her friends on the phone, about how beautiful Emily was now that she had come back. When Emily was in the room, she sputtered and left. Sorry, Mom said at her doorway later, the plane of her right shoulder visible from my room. Sorry I love you so much and can't contain it.

Today, when Mom comes home from work, she mutters a Hello, as if Emily had never left. When Emily hugs her, she blinks, caught unawares, and hugs her back. She makes dinner, spaghetti and green salad, and we sit around the table and twirl our forks to the sound of the old wall clock's tick. Mom says nothing, looks down at her plate, chews absentmindedly. Dad's seat stays empty, tucked evenly beneath the table's edge.

That's the darkest I've ever seen your hair, Mom, Emily says. Going natural?

Mom summons a weak smile. Just haven't been down to the salon in a while, I guess. On her right ring finger, twined around her fork, the nail is split down the center. She picks at it every now and then with her opposing thumb.

When she finishes eating, a painful slow bite at a time, she stands and says, I'm glad you're back, Emily. She leaves her plate in the sink and goes upstairs. I stand to do the dishes, take Emily's plate from her when she finishes too.

She heads toward the stairs, but stops, spins around, asks about Dad.

I ask, What about him?

He's still not here, she says.

His car is missing from the garage. In the early days of this, the telltale rumble of the garage door beneath our second-story bedrooms was my sign of his arrival. Then he started parking outside, letting himself in through the front door. When was the last time he said something I remembered, something more than hello or good-bye?

Sometimes he doesn't come home, I say.

What? she asks, grave. What the hell are you talking about?

A jet passes by overhead—its sharp drone cuts through the window.

For how long? she asks, approaching me at the sink.

I don't know, I say. Sometimes I stop listening to them.

To who?

To Mom. Dad.

What the hell, Suze? she says. She shifts, as if about to storm off, but I grasp at her forearm, pull her next to me.

Sometimes, I say, my nails dug into her arm. Stand with me, I say.

She does—the tension in her arm falls away.

Sometimes, I say, I stand here and shut my eyes and listen to the jet plane and feel the tile under my feet and hear the water in the sink and feel the water on my hands, the heat of it. And sometimes that's all I can do. Because I don't have anyone to talk to anymore. So I sit here and do it on my own. It's calming. See? Look how calm you are now. Look at me. Open your eyes. Look at me. Look at me.

A few years ago, she gave me a stern warning: *Something happens to the boys in high school. Something in them sours, goes bad. You've got to stay away from them, Suze.* She said this with a gravity.

She said this, and then she left me for them—she disappeared into their cars, smiled her sly smile, came home with their smell in her hair and their breath on her neck and a flush on her skin, deep pink, indelible. And then she followed one of them all the way to the coast.

I drop by her room later, when the sky has gone dark—she waves me in, allows me to sit at her side. I want to ask her to swim with me again like we used to, want to start to fix things. I am waiting for the perfect moment, for the last traces of light to be the exact dark blue to bring back memory.

I watch her sift through shirts, transfer some into dresser drawers, some back into boxes. She won't need the thicker ones here, not for the summer, so far removed from the chill winds that coast in off the ocean. She keeps them out anyway, moves on to picture frames filled with old photos of her and her high school friends, back when her hair was streaked through with electric blue. Photos of the family—in one, I had just put eyeliner on for the first time, marker-thick, dark as ink. I want to pull it out of the frame and crumple it up, but it's one of the only photos with me in it.

Outside, the perfect moment has passed, all light fallen away. At some point I notice she has set all the frames down, and then I notice she is sobbing, kneeled between the bed and the dresser, facing away from me, shoulders trembling. I lean toward her, skim her back with my fingertips like we used to as children—I write letters, spell out phrases, inside jokes from childhood, but she doesn't notice. Back then, I was the one who cried, she the one who consoled.

She turns toward me. The moon is out now, and her eyes shine wide.

Get out, she croaks.

My heart crumples like a squashed can. I stand, step out into the hall, shut the door behind me.

When she left, she didn't take everything. She left her plants dotted along the sill. Eventually, when they got sad enough, I took them in as my own, transferred them to my window. Whispered to them at night the way she had, gave them my secrets, my longings. Stroked their strange leaves, shaped like teardrops and tongues. Rolled the pebbles at the bases of their pots between my finger and thumb. Whispered, over the sounds from elsewhere in the house: *I want her to come back, please, let her come back.*

I return from school the next afternoon and find my windowsill empty: she has taken them back. I walk into her room and lift the triptych of small pots into my arms. She catches me as I cross into the hall, as she winds the bend coming up the stairs. She holds the sleeves of her shirt bundled in her hands. Those are mine, she says.

No, I say. You left them behind.

She steps aside, and I move around her, like a river curling around a rock. She throws her window open, leaves the sill bare. The sound of lawn mowers and birdsong skates in on the wind.

Emily appears at my door some two hours later, just when my hand begins to cramp from math homework. She drops a box onto the floor, and some of the socks inside come leaping out and spill across my carpet.

Come help? she says, before disappearing back into her room.

I set my pencil down, scoop the pairs back into the box, carry it down the hall, set it on the end of her bed. She's on the other side of the room, sorting through another box. She has music playing now through her tinny phone speakers. She points to a drawer in the dresser on my side of the room where she wants me to put the socks from my box. She folds pairs of shorts, weighs them against each other, sets two in a drawer, drops four back into a box.

A lot of hot stuff you're leaving out, I say. Like, warm. Like, you must be hot wearing it.

She does a little half-snort, a fake thing, continues sorting her shorts.

Sound continues to filter in through the window, mid-evening sounds now: kids playing in backyards, a firepit rollicking outside, the smacking sound of the flame licking its wood. I decide to seize an opportunity.

Did you and Jamie get married? I ask.

She laughs. No, she says, he never proposed, and thank god for that. Would be a mess to get out of.

She goes silent, turns to her phone to skip past a few songs. A motorcycle zips away on a distant street. She returns to her shorts, continues sorting them into drawer piles and box piles. I think that's all I'll get out of her for today: a valiant effort, I recognize. A thread at a time pulled loose, till eventually I'll have her unspooled, eventually I'll have her back. I'm OK with that pace, that fate.

So I'm surprised when she speaks again.

He realized he didn't love me anymore, she says. And that was the end.

Just like that? I ask.

Just like that.

When Mom comes home from work, she passes the open bedroom door, peers in on us. She's already kicked her ankle boots off and she's got them clasped in her hand. I've moved on to a box of office stuff, which I'm unloading into Em's desk drawers.

How was work? I ask.

Good, Mom says. For a moment, her face is warm, whole. Good.

Then, she disappears, recedes back into herself—that light winks out. She continues on down the hall. I think, *I'm missing something too*, and the words almost leave my mouth, but she's too far now to hear.

Emily says she won't swim. Just like that, the flittering bug of my hope squished beneath her heel. I wanted to do what we used to do, swim laps in the giant pool at the Y, sit in the sauna, talk about everything.

Why don't you just go swim in the creek? she asks.

I want to swim with *you*, I say, reddening. The whimper in my voice, the creak in my throat: suddenly I'm six years old again, begging Mom for a candy bar in the checkout line.

And you hate the creek, I continue, you hate the slimy rocks and the weeds, you say they're always trying to grab you.

They are, she protests. Well, the creek's better than nothing. She sorts through a pile of T-shirts, pauses, holds one in each hand, and lets them fall atop a box still taped.

There's something beautiful about the water at night, she says.

For a moment, I dream it might happen.

But she sighs. But I'm tired, she says.

I take that as my cue to leave.

You have a lot of clothes, I say.

As I step into the hall, I notice Mom's door cracked open—she normally keeps it closed. She's lying across the bed, tucked beneath a tan blanket, boots strewn across the comforter. She must hear me approach, sense the drifting ghost of me, because she says, Make yourselves dinner. Or go buy yourselves dinner. Nothing for me to make in this house anyway.

The sun ducks behind a cloud, and the light fades from the room—she's now only a dark-haired shadow tossed across the sheets. I pull the door shut the rest of the way, slip out of sight.

Emily told me to stay away from them, but she didn't tell me what to do when they kept on anyway, what to do when their need-dark eyes appeared behind their tinted car windows, what to do when they opened the doors to their empty passenger seats, showed you how the engine purred, what to do when they told you to feel it, to *feel* the engine purr, what to do when they sped off, when they held your thigh, grip skin-tight like a pair of leggings, when their fingers skimmed the thin fray of your shorts, what to do when they asked, and asked, and asked, what to do when they took you to the lake, when you shed your clothes, wore less than you ever had, your skin broken out into goosebumps when the sun went down, what to do when still it wasn't enough, what to do when they asked, and asked, and asked, what to do in the dark car seat, in the dark room, in the dark tool shed, when all their breath smelled the same, felt the same, sour and sticky as raw fish, what to do when they never called afterward and all you were left with was the memory of the feeling, what to do when every *hello-how-are-you* text message was secretly an *I-can't-figure-out-how-to-glue-myself-back-together-and-I-need-your-help* text message, what to do when you had to figure it all out yourself, when you had to make yourself the expert.

Emily leans out her window when the sun goes down. She has known how to remove the flimsy screen since I was in seventh grade. I haven't smoked, but I tell her that I have when she offers the joint to me. I am up for the challenge. I want her to think there is a lot she doesn't know about me. Her olive sweater is so dark against her arm, the lit end of the joint a sunburst at her mouth.

We drape ourselves across her bed, high and hot and dreaming. We stare at the colors that drift across her ceiling from her rotating light. My head swims. My tongue etches at the roof of my mouth, dry as sand; there's a pressure, a warmth that persists in my throat. A twinge in my chest, a lightening, something else I can't narrow down, can't feel out, but know is there. I haven't smoked before, but I've breathed it in secondhand with the boys—in my body, it felt like this, but muted. This is an explosion of feeling. Emily is playing music, something light and flimsy, that folds into the collective cacophony.

Don't look at me like that, she says.

Like what?

Like you hate me.

I don't hate you.

You hate me for leaving.

The song of the crickets sluices over us.

But think about it, Suze: wouldn't you get the fuck out of this place, too, if you had the chance?

It's their most frequent line: *Let's get out of here. Let's get away.* Always that coy finger curling me toward them, always that purr. She told me to stay away from them and then she became them.

Maybe, I think. Maybe I would get the fuck out of this place. But I wouldn't ever leave you behind.

We are awake but we are not here. The sun has started to rise; it happens so early these days. The playlist has restarted for the fifth time. Emily now sprawls on the floor, her hair strewn across the thick carpet. The room smells—eventually we gave up on the window. Streaks of pale pink across a sky still the color of midnight.

Why do you wear such long sweaters all the time? I ask.

I've been so cold lately, she says.

But it's so hot outside. Are you sick?

I don't think so.

You're even sweating. Her hairline glistens, beaded.

I'm so high still, she says, letting loose a wild cackle. She's run back to the window to relight and finish the joint a few times already. I raise a hand as if to cover her mouth, to keep the cackle in: Mom's asleep down the hall. Giggles overcome her and she smothers herself in the carpet, empties her laughs into the floor.

I peel away from her bed, return to my room, drift into sleep. She runs into my room, climbs in with me, nestles into me, wakes me too early: I saw something, she says. In the mirror, high and swaying, she'd seen that she'd lost all her teeth—they loosened from her gums, plopped into her palms like small candies. She says, I keep licking them to make sure they're there; I can't stop licking them.

*

After school I find Emily hunched over in the backyard, hands on her knees, shallow-breathed, wearing a long sweater and those long pants. The fire extinguisher lies in the dirt at her feet. One of the shrubs is half-charred, covered in the extinguisher's powder.

I was just trying to burn a picture, she says. Almost set the goddamn yard on fire.

Oh my god, I say. I drop my backpack.

I'm not even on anything, she says. Just a fucking klutz.

She goes into the house, and I survey the damage, lift the fire extinguisher discarded on its side. I find the photo she'd been burning, wedged between two rocks: I thought it'd be of Jamie and her, but it's an old disposable print of her and Dad. Only two edges of the photo burned and had begun to curl. He is smiling—I'd almost forgotten what his teeth looked like, the little jags of incisor. Her teeth, I notice, are all missing—but it's only when I peer closer that I see she's scribbled over them in pen. She opens the door to come back outside, chugging from a glass of water, and I drop the photo back into the rocks, as quick as if it were still lit.

It becomes a habit. She gets ahold of stronger stuff from an old friend named Mark, who hangs around, swats at me like a mosquito when I get too close—Don't you want to see what the other boys have taught me, I want to ask?—until she makes it clear she wants him to leave. The two of us pass it back and forth, and my head swims like I've plied it with helium until I get cold and climb into her bed; there I swelter, sticking to the sheets. The ceiling fan whirs above us, the thrum of her stereo in our limbs.

In the early hours I feel a sharp pricking at my skin, my arms and my back, through my shirt. I roll onto my side, but still feel it beneath me. I run a hand along the sheet, gather small things into my hand: her teeth. I turn to her, find her awake with palms outstretched, offering me a smile, gummy in the moonlight. Her hands are full of teeth and she lets them fall onto the bed, clatter together.

Suze, she says, Suze, go back to sleep. The teeth are soft now, creamy as silk. She pulls me down next to her, brushes her fingertips over my eyelids, consoles me like a dream.

The next night, it's her fingernails, held out to me, curled up in her hands, small, sharp flower petals.

Then her lashes, the ones we got from Mom, pale and thin, trailed along her fingers. She blows and they scatter, glinting in the light, floating like dandelion seeds.

Then the mane of her hair, held in her hand, elaborately folded and tied, like a swan napkin. I don't see Mom, but I feel her hovering, feel her moving.

The sweater again, long and dark and soft, against my bare shoulder. I imagine what she hides, and it's easy, too easy, because she's right, high school has ruined the boys, and it's ruined me too, shown me the world: I imagine track marks in the creases of her elbows, scars along her forearms, patchworks of bruises, of yellows and purples and blues.

I go downstairs for water, mouth dry and wanting, and find Mom in a nightgown at the far side of the table. She smiles at me, and her teeth are all gone. I rush up the stairs into her room, look around, and find them under Dad's pillow. I shove them into her pillowcase, bring them downstairs, dump them on the counter, try to cram them back in, to fit them where they've fallen from, but I can't figure out the sequence. Somehow her mouth has shrunk, or her teeth have grown. She stands and moves into the kitchen, pulls all the glassware to the floor. It explodes at her feet—she steps in its shards, gathers slivers between her toes, pulls more down. Mom, I say, Mom, stop. She bends, picks up fragments of glass, attempts to fit them where her teeth were. Her mouth is again smaller, the orifice is closing up, faster now, until her nose gives way to smooth chin, and I can't remember what came before. Her voice still slips from her somehow: *This is no longer your house!* I hear her scream, though she has no mouth to scream with. *This is no longer your house!*

In the morning, Emily and I clean up the glass on the kitchen floor before I leave for school. Mom's asleep in her bed, turned away from the door, curled into a ball. We sweep up the shards, run the vacuum, wipe the floor with wet paper towels. Then again, all three steps. Still I avoid the kitchen, take careful steps to minimize foot-falls.

I hear Emily in her room when I'm finishing a sweep: Where's Dad? she asks. Where the fuck did he go?

What do you mean? I ask.

He was here, she says. Last night. Hence all the glass.

No, it was me down there, I say. With her.

Emily looks at me like one of my ears has fallen off.

No, she says. You were asleep up here the whole night. He came back at midnight, and we were both up here. There was shouting. Glass.

My brain attempts to wrestle with what she's said.

I was high but I wasn't *that* high, she says.

I'm readying a line of defense, remembering how lifelike it all was, but I hear the shriek of the school bus's brakes from down the block. I dart for the stairs, sprint toward the stop. All day I remember the night, feel it kicking around in me.

Early that evening, Emily offers me more, and I shake my head. I don't like this stuff, I say. She dozes off next to me, russet hair in her eyes. But the secondhand smoke washes over me, though the desk fan's pointed toward the window to push all the smoke out, and eventually I reach for the joint and take a hit.

We start to doze off together. I want to ask her, What was the ocean like? Did you lose yourself in its undulations, or did you get used to it after a while, forget about it? I could never get used to it—it would bring me to my knees every day.

Floating in and out of sleep, I open my eyes to find Emily and Mom screaming at each other, the way they used to in Emily's worst senior-year days. The ends of Mom's hair have gone wiry, hanging in her eyes, obscuring her face.

You can't just let this happen, Emily says, into the hall; her voice pings around in the dark stairway: *You can't just let this happen.*

He's not coming back, Mom says. *He's not coming back*: little assaults of sentences, tangled in the ceiling fan, washing down over me again and again.

Even through the argument, I'm smiling, lax, unfocused—Emily is back, she's *back*, and Mom is lively, animated, filling the house with her shouts, and everything is as it was. Dad's on his way home from work, he'll be here any minute now, won't he?

I drift off and wake up again, find Emily and Mom crouched over me on the bed, pulling my teeth from my mouth, too. There's no pain, only the soft pads of their fingers, the elixir of their smiles. They are so gentle with me, no need for speech.

The car, the car, in the back, in the dark, touch the fog, the hands splitting me apart, *Is this all right?*, you have to be broken open before you can be reassembled, how pain radiates, how it refracts, but at the same time how pleasure spreads, shoulder blades on the cool comforter almost like cold creek water, almost like night swimming, ceiling fan almost like breeze shifting the trees, ears beneath the surface, all you hear is under, no words from Dad, no gentle leveled apologies, no shouts from Mom, no desperate guilt-trip grieving barbs, no roots grown out dark, no nightgowns, no olive sweaters, no nothing.

Emily sips from a bottle of vodka and doesn't flinch. It's Friday, and I'm staring down the empty expanse of the weekend, wincing at the burn in my throat. It doesn't get easier, even when we've downed half a bottle between us. Mom's gotten in the bath—I've listened as she's turned on the old radio, put on one of her blues CDs, the way she does to prepare for a long soak. I heard the clinking of the glass, the slow slip into the tub, the light hum of pleasure at the warmth of the water. She never drank in the bath, warned both us girls against it. She does many things now that she used to dismiss with nevers.

I saw something today, Emily says, on my way home from Mark's.

Mark, the source of the weed that spins my head around, the vodka that simmers in my gut. As she tells me, her breath smells of alcohol and mint.

What? I ask.

Her eyes are clouded with anger. Dad's car, she says. I'm pretty sure. Same tree sticker and everything.

My stomach churns: I haven't seen him in a week, only heard his measured voice float into the room and jolt around a bit. Where? I ask.

That's the real kicker, she says: at Mrs. Giulietti's house. My third grade teacher.

She was mine too, I say.

At the school down by the creek. She lived close enough to walk every day, wore sundresses until it got too cold, long billowing scarves, always smelled like jasmine. Had twin boys, thin and blond, in my grade; I'd kissed one of them in middle school, along the baseball fences. Two blond boys, and no husband, not anymore. We'd all seen the social media posts with GoFundMe links for medical expenses, and we'd all noticed when they stopped.

I wonder if his car's still there, she says. I wonder if he's there right now. I wonder if Mom knows.

A bird coos outside the window, long and slow.

Let's go look, she says. Let's go find him.

I say, I don't know if that's—

What? she says. Eyes held to my throat, hands balled, she seems unstoppable. She was like this, once, this constant overspilling.

All right, I say.

C'mon. She grabs her keys, pulls me down the stairs.

Out in her car, the seatbelt burns me, the hot silver of the buckle. Emily pulls hers over her long-sleeves, starts the car, and we descend down the hill. The vodka sloshes in my stomach.

The look on her fucking face, she says, when she sees me—

Sees us, I say.

Sees us, she corrects. She cranks the windows down—the air outside still swells with heat. Fuck, she says, I just wanna take this fucking sweater off.

Then do it, I say.

I can't, she says.

I'll hold the wheel, I offer, extending a hand toward it.

She swats me away. No, leave it alone, I just can't, she says.

I stay silent, wait for her to explain. She cranks the crackling radio.

She speeds down the main road that parallels the creek until we near the Giulietti house and she pulls into the long driveway. There, on the right side, the telltale Subaru with its tree sticker on the right side. Those are his plates, I say.

Fuck this house, she says, throwing her middle fingers everywhere. Fuck these giant trees, fuck these stones, fuck these fucking handprints in the cement, how fucking corny is that.

The sun is low on the horizon and it glows in the wide panes of the windows, fuzzy orange against the blue of the curtains.

Emily leaps from the car and storms toward the porch.

Fuck these double doors! she shouts back to me, still at the car.

I bolt to catch up with her, watch her pound at the doors, painted blue, framed in white.

I think of her teeth, wish I could reach in and pluck them all out—maybe then the words would spill from her less easily, her gummed-up sounds.

Mrs. Giulietti is at the door now, gone pale. Emily, she says, what are you—

Where is he? Emily asks.

Where is who? Mrs. Giulietti counters. She's using her library voice, like she's pulling us aside at the entrance from the elementary hallway, lowering our volume to respectful levels. Her sundress swishes around her knees, her feet bare. Still, all these years later, she radiates calm and quiet, but Emily plows forward.

His car's in the driveway, Emily shouts, you know fucking who.

Jenna? we hear from inside. Everything all right?

The door squeaks open wider and he's there, in the green chair along the far shelf-lined wall. He's wearing his deep green sweater, his favorite, the one he saves for cloudless days, perfect days. The same color as Emily's—disgust washes over her as she notices.

He looks, for the first time, like he belongs somewhere. He looks at Emily like someone he hasn't seen since he was in high school, whose name is just there at the tip of his tongue. All the vodka in me threatens to come up and out.

Emily pushes past us, teeters toward him. What the fuck, she slurs. The twins, I notice, have emerged from their rooms, stand at the low threshold of the hallway. Dad has stood and approached, hands raised in placation, and Emily shoves him hard. He topples, lands on his hip. Mrs. Giulietti lets out a pained noise. Emily, that's enough, she barks.

Fuck you, Emily shouts. You men, she continues, standing over Dad, you men think you can waltz in and out of families, think you can just fuck and fuck over anyone you choose. *You have a family.*

Mrs. Giulietti's brain blinks in and out behind her eyes.

You can't just fucking *leave* us, Emily implores. Her glare, pelted at Dad, could've set him alight.

I came back, she continues. I came back.

She turns from him, on the floor, hands at his lower back, and blows past our former teacher, leaves the house. There are tears in her eyes. Let's get out of here, she shouts back at me.

I look at Mrs. Giulietti, at Dad, at the twins—I feel Mason's lips on mine, feel his hands on me, though he never touched me, not like the others, I feel it all here again, I see Mrs. Giulietti's violet check marks on my math exercises, watch the back of Dad's head as he approaches the door, watch myself as I turn to follow Emily.

Susie, Mrs. Giulietti says as I pass.

It's Suze, I say, rushing to meet Emily at her Toyota before she leaves me behind, caught in her spiraling storm.

The fucking nerve of that woman, Emily says, careening back toward the house. I want to ask her to slow down but can't move my mouth, my sloths of lips. I lull my tongue around my mouth to make sure my teeth are intact. I always hated her as a teacher, she says.

I think of her blue loops of pen on the whiteboard, her favorite yellow sundress, the pale ribbon she used to pull her hair back. The way she called me Silly Susie, the way I had in our alliteration exercise on the first day of school, and said it with such affection.

At the sudden sight of a bird diving into the headlights, Emily says Fuck, loses control of the car—it veers off the road, plummets into the ditch beside the street. My shoulder slams into my door, my head mere inches from kissing the glass. The car falls still and Emily takes the keys out, lets them fall to the floor. Long grasses tickle the bottom of my window. I rub my shoulder, wince at the pain that radiates out from it.

Fuck! she shouts. She pounds the steering wheel, slams her forehead against it, the balls of her hands.

She settles, quiets. We sit there for a few minutes, watching the last light slip out of the sky. She looks out my window, toward the forest line. Then she begins to laugh.

Wanna swim? she asks, and the world opens once more.

We stand at the side of the creek, the two of us. The air is sticky and hot; my shoulder thrums with pain when I lift my arms to pull at my shirt. When the tight-woven neck ensnares me, Emily helps me with the rest, tears me free. I slip my sandals off, leave them with my shirt. Emily stumbles, pulling at her arms, her legs.

Fuck this green sweater, she says, I'm gonna burn it.

She rips it off, her long pants too, and stands in her bra and underwear. In the near-dark, I strain to look at her skin, dotted with moles. My chest squeezes—I'd forgotten them, the patterns of them. She steps into the water, a cautious foot at a time.

So fucking slimy in here, she says.

I watch the current rollick, watch the ice-blue light bounce off it.

Fuck him, she says, *fuck* him. I got the fuck out of there, Suze, I got out. But I still hear his voice in my head, saying horrible things. I can't even look at myself sometimes. I want to hide.

A kestrel calls out overhead. I think of Mom and Dad, their back-and-forths—*Just another match*, Mom always said afterward, like they'd just stepped off the tennis court. Always with a dismissive smile, and always afterward, a retreat into herself, a thin sheet draped between herself and the world.

As Emily speaks, she turns to face me and the moon illuminates the water behind her, the tops of her shoulders, the wicked dark of her hair, the rest of her fallen away to silhouette.

There was another woman, she says. She lets that float on the current for a while.

But that's not it, or that wasn't all of it, she continues. Sometimes, people will tell you horrible things. And when you find out who those people are, you get the fuck away from them.

She sinks into the water, all the way.

I remember her screaming matches with Mom.

Is that why you left us? I ask. Beneath the surface, she doesn't hear. The current splashes back.

I haven't stepped into the creek yet, but when I do, every muscle in me seizes at the cold. She stands to meet my eyes, wipes my cheeks clear. Why are you crying? she asks.

Her skin, her soul, bared to me—at last, I know I have her back.

You don't deserve any of it, I say.

Oh, Suze, she speak-sighs, like I've gotten mud on new white shoes. It doesn't matter what we deserve. Shit just happens to all of us.

Turned away from me, she stands, and from behind, she looks like Mom—the same slopes of her shoulders, the same shape of her head. I imagine the blues CD having come to an end back at home, the bathwater gone lukewarm, and Mom rising from the water, wrapping herself in a towel.

But Emily sinks back into the stream, allows herself to drift five, ten feet down. Her dark hair's plastered down onto her shoulders, and a giggle bubbles out of her. The current could carry me forever! she shouts. The moon catches on her teeth.

MURMURATIONS

It's around here somewhere, the old thing, ticking away, mouse-qui-
et. Vivian follows the old advice, wonders about the last place she
saw it. She sets her hands at the wall to feel for its slight knock,
kneels in the living room to look beneath the sofa, hunts around in
the dark pockets between the cushions. She follows the baseboards
at the room's perimeters, thinks it may have rolled a bit when it fell.
She checks the linen closet between the folds of cloth, the bathroom
counters and drawers, the floor of the tub, thinking maybe it had
stoppered the drain; the kids' bedrooms, now guest bedrooms, long
vacant, never guested. When she rounds the corner to the living
room, a commercial comes on the TV with the sad blinking caged
puppies, and she thinks maybe a new one has started to grow in her,
but she reaches around inside her ribs and, no, she is still empty.

She keeps watch over the bulbs she planted in the fall, thinks it may have slipped in among them by mistake. Because how long has it been, really, since she felt its tickering? How many months since she's felt its life in her? She doesn't know. She waits for arteries and veins to reach from the ground, but what emerges is only green, only stem. Eventually tulip petals appear from inside the folds, velvety purple, and kiss the bottom of the windowsill, the edges of the concrete steps.

Vivian checks the floor of her car, rummages around in her handbag. Doesn't check the laundry room, can't bring herself to enter. She sits at the kitchen table, panting.

She wonders if maybe it rolled into Heath's grave the day of the burial, beating while his had been stilled. But she isn't about to go dig that up.

Her daughter, Charlotte, comes to visit in the afternoon, after dropping the children off at their father's. She hears the car pulling into the driveway, the engine clicking off, as she sits at the table. Always trudging forward, that one—Vivian doesn't know where she got it from.

In childhood, when she fell and skinned her knee, she stood and kept moving, let the blood run down to her socks, coagulate to a maroon crust. Colin was the one who cried, who milked the pain, looked for sympathy. Now Charlotte is successful in architecture, dresses more nicely than Vivian ever has. She comes to the house not to police Vivian, but to keep her moving—were it not for her weekly visits, sometimes with the children and sometimes alone, Vivian would have fallen into a slump and never risen.

Vivian decides to make blueberry pancakes and eggs—the fruit in the clamshell is sour-faced, on the verge of molding, and she doesn't want to waste it.

After brief hellos, Charlotte perches on a stool, shows Vivian photos of the grandchildren on their recent waterpark trip. In one photo, Charlotte's son's teeth are bared in terror, his inner tube at a steep decline on the water slide. Vivian treasures this. After a while, Charlotte talks about work, and then she gets on to ranting about her ex-husband—something about Vivian makes her fall open, makes it easy for her to get to the real dark heart of the thing.

And it isn't long before she's going in for the real questions.

"When are you going to come with me to visit Colin?" she asks.

"Will you get the syrup out of the fridge?" Vivian asks. There are two bottles, the good stuff and the Log Cabin. Charlotte sets them on the kitchen island, each on its own square of white tile.

Charlotte asks the question again. "You can't stay away forever," she says.

Vivian flips a pancake and it sizzles; she pours the whisked, streaky eggs into the battered pan.

"He keeps asking about you," Charlotte says.

"The butter, too, if you would," Vivian says. "On the door. So it can warm up a bit."

"I know where the butter is," Charlotte says. From her stool, she watches her mother stir the eggs, low and slow, methodical, as she'd always liked to. Vivian knows she itches to turn up the heat, to stir more vigorously.

A blueberry, pressed too hard beneath her spatula, bursts like an organ, its inky juice spreading in the solidified batter.

"Seriously," Vivian says, "the butter."

Charlotte stands, pulls a stick from the fridge, sets it on the counter between the syrup bottles, and approaches her mother, cups her left shoulder with her hand, lays her head on her right. Her fragrance, Vivian notes, is soft and sophisticated, her body warm and close. The two of them had pulled Charlotte's loose teeth out in this kitchen, tied floss to the refrigerator door and slammed it shut. They dyed her hair in this sink, Charlotte bent beneath the faucet, Vivian's protective gloved hand at her forehead.

"Have you even sent back the visitation form?" Charlotte asks.

Vivian swallowed, thinking of it in the junk drawer, among invoices and receipts, screwdrivers and loose batteries.

"Have you even filled it out?"

"Why are you pushing so hard on this?" One side of the pancake, she notices, is burnt, smells ghastly—she scoops it up with the spatula, transfers it to the large plate, scoffs at it. She pours some more batter, listens to it sizzle. Counts to ten in her head, a number for each breath.

Charlotte backs away, returns to her stool at the island. "I don't know," she says, "I just…."

Vivian's eyes have gone dour. "Charlotte, I don't know if I'll ever be able to forgive him."

"I'm not asking you to forgive him," Charlotte says. "But talking to him would be a start."

Vivian stirs the eggs, counts back down from ten alongside her breaths. She turns off the burner, divides the eggs across the two plates, scoops the unsalvageable pancake into the trash, piles the other ones, the good ones, onto their plates, three for each.

"How can you look him in the eye?" Vivian asks.

They are at the edge of a conversation they've had many times before, an argument that never resolves cleanly, a dialogue they've learned to let go of before they enter into it. And Vivian knocks over the cup of viscous egg leftovers, asks Charlotte to grab her a dish towel. The counter floods with yellow-orange, and Charlotte heads for the laundry room.

"No," Vivian says, promptly, in her mom-voice, and Charlotte stops in her tracks. "The drawer right there, I've moved them."

Charlotte reaches for the drawer at the edge of the countertop, and when Vivian confirms, she pulls out a clean towel, hands it over. Vivian sops up the egg liquid, gives Charlotte a terse thanks.

Charlotte carries her plate to the dining table, and Vivian follows with hers. They eat in quiet—Charlotte opts for the nice syrup, Vivian for the Log Cabin. Charlotte's tastes have evolved beyond what she'd grown up on, what Vivian had made for her; Vivian tries to keep things around the house that Charlotte likes now. Though Charlotte still dresses her eggs in ketchup—halfway through her meal, she slips to the fridge, pulls the bottle out, sheepish, and returns with it hidden behind her back. They play a guessing game with it: what could it be, hot sauce, a jar of olives, shredded cheese? Vivian makes a gesture of false surprise when Charlotte reveals the red bottle, squeezes a dollop out atop her eggs.

The red color, so stark against the dark wood, reminds her of the thing she can't find, the thing she'd torn the house apart to look for before Charlotte had pulled into the driveway. She bends her head, now, listens for it around the room, attunes her hearing to the vents and the walls and the stovetop burner clicking. No use. She cuts another piece of pancake, chews it, and a bit of sour blueberry spreads across her tongue, quivers her eyelids.

"You OK today, Mom?" Charlotte asks. "You seem distracted."

Vivian thinks of the heart bounding around and swallows her bite. "No more distracted than ever."

"Are you sure you don't want to move back?" Vivian asks as Charlotte makes her way out the front door, passing a pile of cut-up newspapers.

Charlotte eyes the stack, then smiles tersely at her mother. A relic of a question from young adulthood, before Charlotte was married, before she'd had twins, before she'd had her eventual ex-husband, Nick, when sheer stubbornness kept her out of the house, kept her independent. Before she lost her father, her brother.

Vivian smiles, beams, to hide the fact that she still means the question. Such a strange thing, to wake up to a crookedly empty house.

"Love you, Mom," Charlotte replies. "I'll bring the kids by sometime this week to say hello."

"Oh, how wonderful," Vivian says. "Love you, too." She scoots the newspapers under a chair with her foot, the cut-up front-paged remains of them, and swings the door shut after Charlotte passes through it.

The sun glistens on the windshield as her car backs out the driveway, takes off down the road. Vivian listens till the engine fades, then gathers the newspapers in her hands, carries them out-side to the blue-lidded recycling bin. The lawn looks lovely from the front stoop, green and glinting, dewy. Maybe the kids will want to run through the sprinklers or jump on the trampoline.

For months, Charlotte has insisted that Vivian consider downsiz-ing—the house is simply too large for her alone. Vivian feels the words in the kidney, comes to the defense of the house: how could she give up the children's paint on the bedroom walls, the gas burn-ers Charlotte learned to cook pancakes and boil macaroni on, how could she give up the bathtub Charlotte pickled in, filled with all sorts of scented bubble liquids? The sink her husband, Heath, had trimmed his beard in, the porcelain he'd covered in small shavel-ings? The door frame where Colin had tracked his height, grazed with twenty-five years of tick marks? And the heart, ambling around.

"You don't want the house?" Vivian says, when it comes up.

"You know I just bought a house," Charlotte says. And she had—a modest but gorgeous two-story further in the city, closer to work and closer to the kids' school, which forms a midpoint be-tween Charlotte's house and her ex-husband's. Vivian has been to the house many times—its open, white-walled floor plan, its tight suburban rooms—and prefers to have her daughter and grandchil-dren out at hers.

"You could move out here with the kids."

"Mom, you know it won't happen."

"I could live in the office—we could convert it into a bedroom." Charlotte says nothing.

Vivian swallows. "You wouldn't want me living here?"

Charlotte pauses, clears her throat, on the phone; the sound is tinny, reverberant. "It's my time to do the mothering."

"A mother is always a mother, Charlotte."

"You don't have to worry about me anymore, Mom. I'm not the one you have to worry about."

"Oh, but I do, I always do." Vivian skirts her nails along the surface of the kitchen table. "The worry doesn't ever go away."

Charlotte brings the kids over on Saturday when she gets them back from their father. Ben steps out of the back seat of the car already shirtless, already dressed in the bright blue swim trunks Vivian had gotten him for his seventh birthday. He says hi to her, his Nana, when she meets them at the curb, and runs past her into the grass, through the sprinklers, which she already has running for them. Sadie takes longer to get out of her seat, shuffles up to Vivian and gives her a half-hug. On the verge of turning nine, she has become somewhat ashamed of her brother's actions: turning to watch him flail through the sprinkler head, the corner of her lip quivers in judgment.

Charlotte goes into the house to look for one of her old swim-suits—she's forgotten to bring hers—and Vivian waits outside, sips a cup of tea, watches her grandchildren. Sadie eventually caves, goes for the sprinklers too, but each time she comes over, she resists for longer and longer. The air is warm today, the sun sharp against the roof. Vivian sits in shade, but Ben and Sadie squint in the light. She starts to sip from her mug until she realizes, with a sharp hit of dread, what Charlotte will find inside the house. She stands, runs in after her, but it is too late, she has already seen.

Charlotte comes out of the laundry room looking as if she's found a ghost. "Mom," she says, "what in the hell is that?" Vivi-an watches her put the pieces together: the cut-up newspapers by the front door; the aversion to the laundry room; the disengaged, slightly guilty references to Colin.

Vivian doesn't think about it; she keeps the door closed. But Charlotte has opened it, Charlotte has seen it, and so there is no reason for her to pretend it doesn't exist any longer. Just then she thinks she hears something, coming from the room: a ticktock, a ratcheting. She passes Charlotte, barges into the room. She thought she heard her heart, thought she felt its telltale kicking in her ears, but it is not there when she flips the lights on. All she sees, all that is there, is the newsprint, strung up from floor to ceiling, headlines and tightly-packed paragraphs in various fonts and styles, from various sources. Stuck into the wall with pushpins and, eventually, when she ran out, staples; taped across the top surface of the washing machine, and the window, those pages against glass yellowed by sun; SON INDICTED IN NEWSOM CASE flutters against the wall.

"I don't need to talk to him," Vivian says, looking around at her handiwork. NEWSOM LAWYER BACKS OUT, just above the light switch. *This morning marks another crucial development in the case forming against Colin Newsom.* "I understand everything already. I've been listening."

"No," Charlotte says. "You haven't listened to him, you've never listened to him. You've listened to what everyone else says about him, as always, but you've *never* listened to *him*." The tape at the base of NEWSOM SON FOUND GUILTY comes unstuck from the wall. Charlotte storms out of the house, and Vivian calls for her to wait. She gathers her children, says something about Vivian not feeling well and that they have to leave. Vivian stands at the threshold of the door and watches them pack up, watches them leave. Before he climbs into the van, Ben turns to the house and looks at the glass door; she knows he can't see her, given the bright reflection, but his eyes are heavy, searching. He finally turns and enters the car, and the family backs out.

Vivian can't let go of Charlotte's words. *You've* never *listened to* him. She remembers pretending to be asleep when Heath rose from the bed in the midnight hours, remembers the darkness, the blankness of Colin's eyes in the morning, the way he sometimes blinked back to reality, missed that he was being spoken to because he had been somewhere else. Colin, sitting silently in the car after asking for her to pick him up from school—he was never a quiet kid, always storming with rage or sorrow or joy, so when he was quiet she knew it was because he was trying to hold something in. What he said, when asked why he'd requested a ride from his mother: *Dad's not a good person.* How she slammed her foot on the brake, pulled the car over, said, *Don't ever say that about your father, he raised you, he's a good man, he has always provided for you, don't ever speak of him that way.* And Colin looked at her with fear in his eyes, bright and shining, but also disbelief, like he was set in his convictions and they couldn't be shifted by any winds.

She remembers disregarding his long showers, his rough skin afterward, scrubbed pink. Looking around the kitchen table, counting four heads, including her own. Thinking, *At least we are all together, at least we are surviving.*

She calls Charlotte a few hours later and is, unsurprisingly, met by her voicemail greeting. "I'm going to fill out the visitation form," Vivian says after the tone, "and put it in the mail. I should be cleared in a couple weeks." Before she signs off, she apologizes. For what, she can't specify, but the word rings true in her mouth.

A crash sounds in the room at the top of the stairs, Charlotte's old room. She signs off hurriedly—which will, to Charlotte, come off as an emotional rush-through—and bursts up the stairs. At the top, she is panting, but she swings the door as wide as it will go. She thought she was going to find the thing at last, thought it'd present itself to her by lying at the edge of the bedspread, but nothing is disturbed, save for a photo frame that'd tipped onto its front. She rights it, straightens it—a photo of Charlotte, Nick, and the kids, back when they'd signed off on the house. In the photo, Ben is newborn, his head plastered with soft down, and Sadie is nearly a toddler, standing on her own, clinging to the knee of Nick's pant leg. The photo was taken days before Colin's trial began. Both Charlotte and Nick seem so calm, so happy, though the following months would tear them apart, they would tear everyone apart.

She returns to the kitchen, begins to fill out the form, includes in the envelope a check for twenty-five dollars, a background check fee. One of the questions on the form asks if she desires to visit the inmate. Had she filled out the form prior to today, a Yes answer would have been a lie or, at best, tangled in a knot alongside other stormy feelings; today, she scratches the pen across the Yes bubble with vigor till she tears through the thin sheet of paper.

Charlotte, after a few days of storming, calls and offers to drive Vivian to the prison when she is cleared for visitation. Vivian has not spoken to Colin in months, has not seen his face or heard his voice anywhere other than on the nightly news. Even in the news clippings strewn around the laundry room, she has taken care to cut the photos of him away from the text, to discard them with the rest of the paper. Headings and text bodies only; no photographs, nothing to pull her toward impartiality. (Though isn't the mere mention of his name, she has to wonder, enough to make her impartial? On some level, yes, but it's nothing like the gut-sway she feels when she sees his photographs, the sudden leap of her heart is nowhere near.)

For days, weeks before the visitation date that is set, her stomach roils with anxiety. She almost calls off the whole thing to get the horrible feeling to go away. But she has made up her mind, she is set in her course of action: she isn't going to call the thing off, isn't going to ignore the wound because it has festered, it has deepened and widened and multiplied its infection, and she has spent far too long turning a blind eye to it.

She also makes a list of real estate agents from the Yellow Book beneath the kitchen sink. Not because she's made any decisions—but because she's entertaining the idea, curious what the place is worth, what the process might be like. The agent Vivian and Heath had used to buy their house all those years ago also guided Charlotte through the purchase of hers—her last sale before she retired. Thus Vivian was on the market. She was listening, she was considering.

And maybe, if she hadn't found the heart by now, she was never going to. She'd gotten used to the cavity.

She thinks of the last day of Heath's life, back when medical personnel thought he was going to live. Back before his sudden turn for the worse. Vivian sat next to him at the hospital, held his wrinkled hand, felt the veins of it, the ligaments, shifting beneath his skin. She remembers she couldn't say a single word, wasn't able to find any. She hadn't slept in days, hadn't drank water in as long, and it hurt to run her tongue across the roof of her mouth. Instead of speaking she clutched his hand, folded his fingers flat onto his palm, and squeezed, squeezed, as hard as she could. Till she was sure she had broken the thing entirely, folded it in on itself, and blood would be spurting from it, a fresh fountain of a wound. But she opened her eyes and his hand was fine, it was there, it was its same pallid wrinkled self, and she was full of questions she couldn't ask, full of questions she'd never get answers to, full of a darkness she couldn't let out. That was the last time she had seen him, the last thing she'd done to him while he was alive. She had squeezed so hard, dug his nails into the ball of his own thumb till she thought she'd cut skin. He had been comatose; she had wondered how the pain appeared in his mind, if not in words, if not in conscious thought, what the colors of it were behind his eyes.

The day of the visitation, her heart is in her throat. She's wearing prison-approved attire and Charlotte, too, is dressed conservatively, as if the two of them are headed to a business dinner. Though Charlotte isn't visiting today: perhaps she's dressing in solidarity. Vivian meets her in the driveway, buckles her seatbelt, and they are off. The ride out to the prison is long and sparse on a straight, flat highway, halfway between their city and the next. She can see the prison's fencing, the tan buildings poking out above from miles away. She counts down slowly in her head, dreads the end, but knows it must come, knows it has been a long time coming.

Charlotte is quietly smiling, pleased with herself, as if the victory is hers. She hugs her mother at the doors, says she'll be waiting outside for her. She'll be back next week, Vivian knows, for her own visit.

Vivian enters the building, checks in. She waits, waits, her blood leaden in her arms and legs.

When he finally rounds the corner, she doesn't recognize him, at least, not the version of him she'd last seen—he's as thin as he was in high school, tan jumpsuit sagging over his shoulders. He approaches her, hovers around the table she has chosen. He, like her, must be unsure where they stand. Eventually he sits across from her, his hands flat on the table. She takes one of them into her own, holds it, strokes his knuckles with her thumb.

She is unsure what to say, where to start. Unsure how to mend the months. So she asks the only thing that comes to mind, the only thing that matters: "Why did you do it?"

He cocks his head, narrows his eyes. He wants her, she figures, to say it.

So she tries—stumbles through the opening words, tries and tries again, till she gets it right, till its sounds hang in the air between them: "Why did you kill your father?"

And she sees it there, figures it an illusion, tries to blink it away, but it remains: there, between his teeth, beating, beating. It is where it has always been, in his mouth like an orange slice. She reaches out for it, but he bites down, till it pops, runs red.

WHAT IS THE NATURE OF THE DANCE CALLED MEMORY

Anne Carson said that a wound gives off its own light. So too does love, which lit me from the inside.

The house was a Craigslist affair: three rooms, each independently sought out. The first, at the front of the house, was claimed by someone named Sam, who lit it with gaming screens, punctuated it with keyboard clacks and gun blasts, unloaded magazine after magazine with the remote. At all hours of the day: breakfast time, those hulled-out shells hitting the floor. Mid-afternoon, sonorous footsteps in video-game corridors. Dinner, tinny radio communications, victory music. I never saw much of Sam.

*

In the middle was my room, with two boxes of spine-broken books, a wingback chair, a single beachside postcard tacked to the wall, a ceiling fan with no chain. Caught in the highest setting, always whirring. Its whir bled into my dreams.

And then yours, the back-corner bedroom. A giant antique lamp, long billowing curtains. Books everywhere—you were a long-haul student like me, swamped with work, no time for games or parties or partners or fun. All fun was self-imposed, labeled as self-care. In the name of prolonging life. I only saw you when one of us was coming or going. We both liked to rot in a room and do our work.

I had been holding my head above the pillow and whispering into the pillow and wondering when my life was going to start. I had been doing this for some time now.

At first your kindness was gestural. A few words in the kitchen while I was segmenting citrus. A polite bullet-pointed recap of the day when you first tucked inside the front door. It was civility—not friendship, but friendly. It was a face to look at instead of a screen, or a wall, or a slice of tree. It was so many things at first.

Then it crept into the genuine. You were a philosopher but you knew the esoteric poet I was studying. (Were our fields, I wondered, ever so different?) You knew off the top of your head what she said about love. You found your favorite poem in my collected edition, tick-marked it with your blue pen, and when you left I studied your tick-mark in the stove light. You hadn't asked, you had just done it.

While I cooked you stood at the lip of the counter and asked me questions—about my dissertation on love poems, about the color of my soul, about how I kept friendships, about the sandwich I could eat every day for the rest of my life. And when I answered you listened, you didn't look away.

People had always taken me at face value. Nobody had ever wanted to know me before. I knew myself: I was tired, my undereyes saddened with bags, I was hungry and I burned with anxiety, stomach constantly acroak, I was empty, I couldn't sleep, I was half-alive, pulse a suggestion of a thing because where was the real living, I wanted to drive to the ocean, I was closed, I was full of love and starved for it, I had peeled all my fingernails to the quicks, I was restless, I went through phases of happiness and crushing sorrow, I was broken, I was breaking, I was hopeless, I was hoping, but above all I was lonely. I think this loneliness accelerated my wounding, made me reach for a cure.

We read and studied and wrote, and I ate when I felt empty, and then we found ourselves in the living room asking each other questions until we found we had been asking each other questions for hours.

You didn't like answering the questions you asked me in return but I said it was only fair.

Periodic long check-in calls. Anything with turkey. Rose quartz (interesting).

When it was cool enough we ventured out to the porch and listened to the neighborhood. We watched somebody moving into the house across the road. Through the open blinds we watched them carry box after box, bin after bin. We talked about the moon on the rear window of their car over there, how it glowed, shifted, like it was alive.

You asked if I thought it was silly, what we were doing. Working and studying and analyzing and writing ourselves to death. It was 2:37 a.m. and your splayed limbs constellated the couch. I sat on the floor, which I was fond of doing.

Yes, I said. I watched the pages of my book shift beneath the ceiling fan. But, I continued, it makes me happy. Or at least I have been conditioned to think it will make me happy.

What are we doing? you asked.

So we went and got fast food and brought it back. We rebelled. From the front of the house we could see Sam's screens flashing bright in the windows. We brought our food inside and ate it on the floor, emptied ketchup packets onto napkins, dumped fries into grease-stained burger boxes. The food went caustic in my stomach after a few minutes, but I watched you chew your burger, slow eater you were, and it was like you were thinking through a very complex math problem or trying to remember an old classmate's name.

All of this was a thing I elected never to tell you. You wouldn't know what to do with it. But I could hold the feeling inside and keep it warm there.

You noticed my ailment before I did, while I was caramelizing shallots.

Where's your shadow? you said. You have no shadow.

My face burned; I thought you were being poetic. I wished for a shell to recede into. But I looked down and indeed saw no shadow trailing me. I walked into the living room where, again, I was shadowless. I jumped, crouched, went into tree pose. Nothing.

Your eyes were big. You're glowing, you said.

A wound gives off its own light. You slit me open and turned me to wound.

You shone your phone's flashlight on me, figured me hollow. You poked me, figured your finger would pass right through. You pricked me with a sewing needle, figured me an inflated thing, full of air. You startled when I let out a yelp and blood bloomed at the spot. What are you? you asked.

My imaginary friend, you joked again and again. My imaginary friend. But I was real, I was so real.

I glowed alone in my room at night. My own light kept me awake—I had to pull a blanket over my eyes to fall asleep.

And why, you wanted to know, was I so deliriously happy?

Every time you asked, a new excuse found its way to me. Feeling like I finally cracked the code of a poem I have been trying to access for a long while. Feeling like I made a breakthrough in a seminar today. Feeling like all this isn't so impossible anymore. Still bounding, still shadowless.

I elected never to tell you, held the words of the feeling inside, but I was legible all the same, I was floating.

*

At the store I walked past a paperweight made to resemble rose quartz, which you had said was your soul color. It was a big stone-like lump, the bottom of which had been cut off, so it was flat. Of course I bought it, set it at the edge of my desk. In the morning the sun struck it just right through the slats of the blinds and it glowed like a horizon.

Very few people noticed the shadow thing. Nobody really looks at people anymore, they are too distracted by their own goings-on. But I began to miss my shadow, the way you miss a thing you have seldom looked directly at. I had taken its presumed foreverness for granted. I missed its long stretch of dark.

Our new neighbor, it appeared, was having a party. Your ears perked up at the thuds of bass, the whirls of chatter, the swirling living room lights, and you left to investigate. I stayed in my room and read through the noise. You came back, hours later, and when you leaned against my door frame I saw that something had happened to you—you wore some new mood, some new feeling. Your eyes were wide and swimming as if the answers to your confusion lay somewhere in the matterless light. Flushed at your face and neck—blooming there.

While I marked up my books I thought of your room, the big lamp, its amber glow like the sun in the earliest morning, the color pale as your soul.

It started slowly and then it happened all at once. You disappeared, again and again—when you went to get the mail, to go for a walk, to take out the garbage. Every time I stood at the window I saw you there, a dot on the lawn across the street, talking to the neighbor. Sometimes on their porch, and sometimes a glow in their front window.

The air conditioning came on, a musty exhale. I wanted you to ask me questions. I could feel myself falling out of your memory.

In early autumn I liked to open my bedroom window to catch the breeze as it passed through, but when the two of you were out there at the curb, I could hear you—laughs cascading over the fence, pure as silt, the volleys of your jokes and retorts—and so I kept it shut, sweat through my clothes, sat beneath the ceiling fan, felt the air move over me.

I saw the neighbor once up close, while walking out to my car— they were at the corner, slipping something into our mailbox. They waved a tepid wave and turned around. Minutes after, when they had gone back into their house, I opened the mailbox. There was a letter for Sam which I would leave on the kitchen table. But there was also a note. I didn't read it, didn't destroy it. Just looked at its bottom and left it where it was. It was signed with a heart and *Caz*.

A darkening occurred. Not only did my shadow return, but it overtook the rest of me—I was hard to spot in any room. I could not see myself in my mirror, I was the absence of light. You returned from across the street and walked right past me, as if the kitchen were empty. Then you turned and squinted at my darkness and said, Is that you?

*

You looked past me, moved around me. Slipped through the neigh-borhood in your sleek way. Here one moment, gone the next—then back, as if no time had passed at all, rosied and lovely and pristine. Like you had finally woken from the long sleep, the one that still had its bedsheets tangled round my ankles.

In my room I looked *up* Caz and learned that it meant destroyer of peace. Its first two letters, its *c* and *a*, were so soft, rounded, but its *z* was so sharp it could have poked a hole in any peace. I would have laughed, if I could have, but I was only a dark soundless thing.

I missed the hot desert of myself. When the light was everywhere I looked. It had pared me away and replaced me with its glow, and now that it had gone, I was vacant.

I hid in my dark room.

You went love-blind. Didn't notice anything till long after it hap-pened. When I receded, you weren't aware, till the third time I left my room and walked to the kitchen, at which point you blinked, waking from a stupor, looked in the direction of my darkness, and said, Where have you been?

Sam came in and out of the kitchen, grabbed a bag of chips, but said nothing. Probably didn't see me.

You didn't understand why I continued to hide. But I hadn't told you about why I had been so buoyant so I couldn't tell you about this part either. Had to hold it inside me too. I was running out of room for unspoken things.

I WANT SOMETHING I CAN NEVER HAVE. I wanted to scream it at you. But to know of its impossibility did not negate the wanting. It only gave it a further sheen of dark.

A couple times I could sense you were on the verge of asking. But you had suspicions brimming on your tongue, suspicions about the origin of my hurt, that you didn't want confirmed. Or so I reasoned as you came home to retrieve a book or two, carried them across the street with you. The table over there was perfect for studying, it caught the light perfectly. The tip of your pencil gleamed in it.

I had thought my life was starting but really it was just turning over. Revealing a new facet of its listlessness.

You still spent some of your moments with me, but you were never really there. You checked your phone again and again waiting for their messages, screen going light dark light dark. I could see their name on you it emanated from you like sweat from your pores C A Z.

Everything shouldn't have hurt as much. But I had changed in the three months I had known you, my days had bloomed open into things that, when held together, resembled a life. And now I was trailing the shadow of the person I had been before.

I wanted to ask, how many times over the months have you felt me almost say it? How many times have you heard my breath hitch, my mouth close around the words as they threatened to escape?

Caz came around for breakfast one day. I passed in and out of the kitchen, but neither of you noticed the shifting light. I wanted so desperately to hate them, but they brought eggs from home, laughed at your jokes, gathered the dishes after you had eaten, set a small vase of flowers at the center of the table, bright yellow, picked from their porch.

It wasn't only the act of loving but the act of killing love. Of smothering its breath.

Of suturing the wound, erasing your traces.

I had enjoyed studying the love poems because they had approximated something I had not known. Reading the words had given me a parallel feeling. But now the words were digging into the skin and ripping at the stitches. I tried to read the collected volume you tick-marked, but the words emerged in your voice.

I would have preferred to leave love to the poets, to the pages. To keep it in the text and out of the body.

Dust gathered on my shelves, on the book tops. It grayed my fingertips.

It was far too late to overhaul my dissertation but I had no interest anymore. Everything I wanted to connect had already been connected, everything I wanted to say had already been said.

I considered knocking at Sam's door to quell my loneliness but I had no interest in video games. And besides we had only ever exchanged a handful of words. I had no energy to start over again, to build something new.

No longer was I all shadow; in a sense, I had come back to myself. But I felt hollowed out in some way. Like I had expelled all the feeling I had within me.

So I sat on the couch and watched the trees shift in breeze. You and Caz sat in the yard and chewed on grapes. You reached up toward the oak branches and the shadow of your arm trailed across the lawn. You had held on to it, managed not to let the feeling destroy you.

Caz said your name and it felt warm and rippling, like laughter.

I had said your name gravely like it was a secret I was finally letting out. You said no one had ever regarded you as seriously. Said it sounded like I was condemning you to some fate. And wasn't I? I was condemning you to love each time I incanted it.

Condemning you to past, present, and future.

Look, faraway, look—there you are. In the shifting light of the distance. In the always.

ACKNOWLEDGMENTS

The stories in this book were written across five years, between 2019 and 2024. Across that span, I was at least twelve different people, with different interests, hobbies, and tastes—as such, I can't possibly thank everyone I need to, but I will try my best.

Thanks, first, to the wonderful people at Split/Lip Press who helped realize my longest-running dream, and who have done it with such care and grace: Kristine, for everything you do, and for fine-tooth-combing through the manuscript, and Caleb, for helping to run the show; Pedro, for pulling my manuscript from the slush and helping me sharpen its edges; David, for the book's beautiful outside and inside; Abby and Gage, for your marketing dynamo.

Thanks to Matt Bell, whose teachings about writing transcend genre, form, mode. We worked very little together on short stories, but everything I write is stronger, leaner, and better on its feet because of you. Thanks to Tara Ison, whose craft lessons have so strongly shaped my work. Thanks to Jenny Irish, who is such a fantastic champion, a generous reader, and a wonderful person. Thanks to Sally Ball, Solmaz Sharif, and Mitchell S. Jackson, for the ways in which you helped me grow as a writer, reader, thinker, and human. Thanks to Justin Petropoulos for keeping my head above water. Thanks to my students, whose lively discussions about writing left me energized.

Thanks to everyone who read versions of these stories across the years: Annie Vitalsey, Warren Glynn, Justin Noga, Chloë Boxer, Tucker Leighty-Phillips, Jules Hogan, Rachel Reeher, Steffi Sin, Christie Louie, Christina D'Antoni, Colin Bonini, Winslow

Schmelling, Arya Naidu, Asna Nusrat, Amber Wardzala, Frankie Concepcion, Haylee Massengill, Maya Chari, Jonathan Danielson, Amy Kitchens. What an honor to learn and grow alongside you.

Thanks to the book's early readers for your kindnesses. I wish I could gather you all around a table and ply you with wine and feed you something delicious, but science has not yet made this teleportative act possible.

Thanks to the hosts of the residencies at which several of these stories were drafted or revised: Dorland Arts in Temecula, CA; Creekside Arts in Eureka, CA; Studio Faire in Nérac, France.

Thanks to the endless musicians whose works fueled my writing—far too many across five years to name here!—but most prominently Grouper (whose title "Headache" I lovingly stole), Nina Simone, Beach House, Sufjan Stevens, Joni Mitchell, Slowdive, Julianna Barwick, Kali Malone, Julia Holter, Ben Howard (same, re: "Evergreen"), and Marcus Fischer (same, re: "Murmurations").

Thanks to the editors of the publications in which some of these pieces appeared previously: *Witness*, *West Branch*, *Quarter After Eight*, *Allium*, *Yalobusha Review*, *Passengers Journal*.

Thanks to the folks at Infusion Coffee & Tea, within whose walls (and on whose patio) I chipped away at several of these stories. (I told you you'd be in here!)

Thanks to Sara Jones, whose love of books fed my own, and whose wisdom has guided me for fourteen years. Thanks to David Nikki Crouse, who spied my tentative footsteps and nudged me down this path. It's fully thanks to your kindness and encouragement that I began to take myself seriously as a writer.

Thanks to friends—all my MFA buddies, hometown folks, undergrad pals, and, of course, my Rileys—for a lifetime of love and support. Thanks to my family—Mom, Dad, D, Ty, Mia—for keeping me going when this dream seemed out of reach, and for never ceasing to believe. I love you.

HAYDEN CASEY is a writer and musician currently living in Phoenix, AZ. He earned a Bachelor's degree in Psychology from the University of Washington and an MFA in Fiction from Arizona State University. His debut novel is forthcoming from Lanternfish Press later this year. His short work has appeared or is forthcoming in *Witness*, *West Branch*, *Bat City Review*, and elsewhere. He teaches writing at Arizona State University, where he was the 2024 recipient of the College of Arts and Sciences Outstanding Instructor Award. Find him at haydencasey.co.

NOW AVAILABLE FROM
SPLIT/LIP PRESS

For more info about the press and titles, visit us at
www.splitlippress.com

Follow us on Instagram and Twitter: @splitlippress

www.ingramcontent.com/pod-product-compliance
Lightning Source LLC
Chambersburg PA
CBHW020018030726
47499CB00007B/2166